The Woman Who Was Not There

Fanny Fanfairly has recently inherited an infamous Victorian brothel house in the centre of Windsor. The house is now run down and empty, apart from the strange wax models – each striking an erotic pose – that inhabit every floor. And Fanny is convinced these models are moving all by themselves...

She asks her friend, high-ranking policewoman Charmian Daniels, for help. But Charmian has little time to ponder on the old woman's bizarre fears, for a London prostitute, Alicia Ellendale, has gone missing following a day trip to Windsor. Alicia has one very distinguishing feature – the stub of a sixth toe on her right foot.

A missing person case would not normally be Charmian's domain – but her bosses are getting twitchy because Alicia was last seen on her way to visit Frank Felyx, a recently retired inspector from their division. What's more, Frank is now refusing to open his door.

Charmian is given the unenviable task of finding the missing woman before the police are dragged into a messy case. And at some point she's still got to sort out the strange goings-on in Fanny's new house...

Then a young boy makes a gruesome discovery on the river bank at Runnymede – a shoe bearing a woman's severed foot...

By the same author

Come Home and be Killed
Burning is a Substitute for Loving
The Hunger in the Shadows
Nun's Castle
Ironwood
Raven's Force
Dragon's Eye
Axwater
Murder Has a Pretty Face
The Painted Castle
The Hand of Glass
Listen to the Children
Death in the Garden
Windsor Red
A Cure for Dying
Witching Murder
Footsteps in the Blood
Dead Set
Whoever Has the Heart
Baby Drop
The Morbid Kitchen

Jennie Melville

The Woman Who Was Not There

MACMILLAN

First published 1996 by Macmillan

an imprint of Macmillan General Books
25 Eccleston Place, London, SW1W 9NF
and Basingstoke

Associated companies throughout the world

ISBN 0 333 66308 X

Copyright © Jennie Melville 1996

The right of Jennie Melville to be identified as the
author of this work has been asserted by her in accordance
with the Copyright, Designs and Patents Act 1988.

All rights reserved. No reproduction, copy or transmission
of this publication may be made without written permission.
No paragraph of this publication may be reproduced, copied or
transmitted save with written permission or in accordance with
the provisions of the Copyright Act 1956 (as amended). Any
person who does any unauthorized act in relation to
this publication may be liable to criminal prosecution
and civil claims for damages.

1 3 5 7 9 8 6 4 2

A CIP catalogue record for this book is available from
the British Library

Phototypeset by Intype London Ltd
Printed by Mackays of Chatham PLC, Chatham, Kent

Part One

Chapter One

Tuesday

A winter's day in Windsor, that ancient town which changed and yet was unchanging. Because of the number of visitors and daily tourists, there was a floating population from which it was easy to disappear. A coach came in from London on an excursion. All the passengers dispersed, reminded by the driver that they must meet him again at the coach station by a certain hour.

When they set off again that evening, one passenger was missing. No one noticed except the driver, who waited for a few minutes then departed. It was the way things went sometimes. He could not remember if the missing passenger was a man or a woman.

At least that was what he said. As it happened, he remembered perfectly well: it was a woman.

Disappearances, but also appearances.

A town in which strange events could happen and where ghosts walked. It was said that on the right nights King George III could be seen leaning out of a window, looking mad and saluting his royal troops who were not there.

And not only ghosts, but even odder, nastier figures were said to be on the move.

*

In Leopold Walk (the Leopold was reputedly the youngest son of Queen Victoria) in the centre of the town, there were four Victorian houses, each narrow, detached, set in a row with one on the corner.

It was a cul de sac, with a high brick wall facing the terrace. Once family homes, for the last thirty years or so each had housed a small business. Number four, at the end of Leopold Walk, held the offices of a small accountancy firm, number three belonged to a husband and wife architectural firm, small but prize-winning. And next door was a computer agency. All three businesses had one thing in common: they were very inward-looking; the men and women who worked there walked down the road or eased their cars into the difficult parking without appearing to have much to do with their neighbours. They passed number one and occasionally thought: odd place; but they shrugged and went on. Not their business.

Number one Leopold Walk was different, it was dusty, shut up and neglected. Empty, yet not empty.

Charmian Daniels, policewoman, looked down upon the diminutive figure walking at her side on the hill near the castle, whose conversation was worrying her; she could see how distressed her companion was. Fanny was talking, but not being quite as specific as she could be. What was it all about?

'Come on, Fanny, tell me more. You said you had to talk to me, and now you're just wringing your hands and weeping.'

'Not weeping,' said Fanny sharply. She had her

pride, and weep in public she would not. A fearful tear in private, yes.

Charmian shook her head. 'Sorry, not weeping, Fanny.' The two women had halted in the crowd of onlookers at the crest of the gentle hill. The soldiers were marching through the town as they did twice a day. They were young and erect and eyes straight ahead. One in particular attracted Fanny's attention.

'Lovely, isn't he?' said Fanny Fanfairly (real name Fanny Fisher). 'I always love a soldier.' She was staring at a tall young man in a bearskin and grey winter uniform, banging a drum as he marched with his companions of the Royal Guard from their barracks to the great castle on the hill. 'Welsh Guards this month. But not as tall as they used to be, guardsmen aren't. Not like they were in my day. They can't get the men.'

A tiny, fragile-boned old lady herself, she looked up hopefully for confirmation.

'So I've heard,' Charmian responded politely.

'Policemen, too,' said Fanny. 'Smaller.' She sounded pleased. Charmian did not answer. We're big enough, she thought.

Charmian had first worked in politics, straight from university, decided it was not for her, and became a copper. She had worked her way up from walking the beat to detective and on and up to becoming a high-ranking officer in charge of SRADIC (Southern Register and Documentation of Crime). She was a powerful woman, with her own investigating staff. She saw all important records of crimes and could initiate her own checks if she so desired.

'Things change,' she said soothingly to her old

friend, wondering how she had become a friend of Fanny, retired tart and brothel owner. Fanny was not ashamed of her past, claiming that she had performed a necessary service well and brought harm to no one. She only wished it had left her richer. 'A working woman,' she had said, 'and not ashamed.'

'I like the Irish Guards best myself,' said Fanny now. 'I always had a weakness for them. Such men, they are.'

You'd know, thought Charmian. Fanny was old and frail now, her bones thin as a bird's and her face lined, but she still applied a bright shine of lipstick, dyed her hair auburn and touched up her eyes with liner and mascara. On her good days she looked ageless. Today she seemed to have shrunk within herself. Charmian knew she was about eighty.

'So what's up, Fanny?' asked Charmian. 'Why did you want to see me?'

Fanny frowned but did not answer.

'And why did we have to meet in the middle of Windsor and not in your house? I would have come there, you know that.'

Once Charmian had lost her cat and Fanny had read the tag round the creature's neck and brought it home. From that meeting a friendship, of a kind, had grown. If Fanny trusted anyone in the police service she trusted Charmian.

'I felt like the open air.'

'Right. Well, the way the wind is blowing, the air is very open.' It was a chill January day with a hint of snow.

'Sometimes you need a woman,' muttered Fanny.

Charmian said gently: 'Is there trouble where you live?'

Down Peascod Street, turn right into Brunswick Street and then a few yards to the left turn right into Adelaide Passage was a row of small early nineteenth-century houses, once the homes of artisans but now prized by the gentry. In one of them, the last of its kind, a theatrical lodging house since the turn of the century, Fanny had a room and a kitchen; she shared a bath with the lodgers as they came and went.

'No, they're good to me there,' said Fanny, her head down.

'So they should be.' Charmian knew the Neederlys who ran it, as the family had done for generations, and knew that they politely accepted that Fanny was a resting, retired performer living on a small income, not the former owner of a brothel in Knightsbridge. 'I was always top of the heap,' Fanny had said once with some pride, 'and could have been rich if I hadn't been such an extravagant piece. And I treated the girls well; one of them married a duke, you know.' Fanny probably had more in the way of savings than she admitted to, and had indeed once been on the boards, but Charmian was doubtful about the duke.

'You know about my inheritance . . . left me by a dear old friend.' It was a statement and not a question, made with a mixture of pride and anxiety. 'I keep an eye on it, you know. Watch it. Regular as clockwork, I am.'

'Sure. You told me.' Several times. And you told everyone who would listen as well. 'I didn't know you kept watch. Is there any trouble with it?'

If Fanny wanted to talk to her about it, then there probably was trouble since Fanny regarded her as a kind of goddess in a machine who could solve problems. She had already sorted out Fanny's pension and the tax on her small investments. On which subject she was far from sure that Fanny had told all the truth, but Charmian knew when to stop digging and leave well alone.

But the inheritance was a strange affair. An old admirer (or so Fanny admitted William Beckinhale had been before old age had removed him from the scene) had bequeathed to her an ancient house in Windsor. Fanny had been exceedingly proud, undecided whether to sell it or move in. The house, she knew, had been neglected for years.

'I went to take a look this week . . . just a check, you know, but I have to wait for probate of the will before it's really mine. But I didn't see why I shouldn't take a look through the windows. And I've gone on doing it. No harm there.'

'Of course not,' said Charmian reassuringly. She wondered where the conversation was leading.

'Besides . . .' Fanny hesitated. 'There had been a sort of a business there . . .'

The road was clearing as the Guards marched into the castle and traffic and pedestrians began to move forward.

'Come along, I'll show you.' Fanny walked forward with her delicate, mincing gait. She always wore high-heeled shoes in which she stepped carefully over the cobbles.

'Wait a minute . . . This business, Fanny?' said Charmian, a wordless question in her voice. She raised an eyebrow.

'No, not that,' said Fanny hastily. 'Not exactly... I'll explain when we get there.'

She led the way across the road which led up to the castle, then through the old Market Street to a narrow turning, Princess Victoria Louise Street. This was Leopold Walk.

Charmian paused at the corner, forcing Fanny to slow down. The street was narrow and cobbled with a high wall on one side and four houses on the other.

'Mine is the one on the corner,' said Fanny. 'Freehold property. All mine.' She sounded gloomy.

'Well, that's lovely. You can sell it. Or live in it.'

'The thing is...' Fanny hesitated, as if she did not know how to put it. 'It has... people in it.'

'Tenants?'

'You could call them that.'

'You can get them out. Ask them to leave.'

'Not this lot,' said Fanny.

Charmian stared at her. 'Come on, Fanny, what is this?'

'They don't walk and they don't talk... I think they move, though.'

The house fronted straight on to the street, three narrow floors with a window on each, detached, with a wild garden behind. It looked as though it shared the garden with the house next door, and the one beyond, although bushes and a ragged hedge suggested there had once been boundaries. At the side of the house was a small barred window which looked as if the ground level had risen and half buried it. Fanny led

Charmian straight up to the front window which gave on to the street. It was curtained, but there was a gap in the curtains.

'Take a look. I did.'

Charmian put her face up to the window. The window was dusty but she could see into the room. It was set out as a dining room with heavy oak furniture, Jacobean or Tudor in style. A man sat at the table and a serving maid leant towards him; he appeared to be touching her waist.

'Wax,' said Fanny. 'Old English kitchen behind, with naked kitchen maid, you can't see that from here. Tudor on the ground floor. Eighteenth century above, Regency, that lot . . . and Victorian on the top floor.'

'It's a museum of costume,' said Charmian.

'You could call it that,' answered Fanny. 'I daresay some did. But not what they went for.'

'You've been inside?'

Fanny produced a key. 'Mr Grange of the solicitors let me have this. He didn't see why not – he's been inside himself and had a look. Surprised him, I think. Did me a bit. The ground floor is fairly mild, but it hots up as you go up the stairs.'

She was opening the front door and motioning Charmian inside. A puff of stale, dusty air, yet still scented with ancient aromas of sandalwood and chypre, mingled with other, stranger smells.

'A private club, I think,' said Fanny, standing still. 'Or a gentleman's amusement for his friends. I don't know if money passed hands. My friend who left it to me said he inherited from his uncle, but I don't know about that.'

'How odd that I've never heard of it.'
'You wouldn't, closed up for years.'
'The police usually know about things.' Not to mention the neighbours, Charmian thought. What a place.
Fanny shrugged. 'Private, like I said.'
Charmian took a deep breath; she didn't know whether to laugh or not. Fanny's inheritance was a kind of judgement on her, and perhaps intended to be so. 'What did your old friend think you would do with it?'
'I don't know. Sell it, use it, live in it.' Fanny started to walk up the stairs. 'Come on, have a look.'
Charmian followed her up the narrow stairway. Ahead, a double door opened.
The Regency room was charming, the furniture, of delicate mahogany and brass, looked genuine. The curving sofa was covered in striped yellow satin, now somewhat faded and dusty.
On the sofa sat a woman dressed in a transparent muslin. She was stretched out in an enticing fashion before the man who sat next to her.
'Dear me,' said Charmian.
'Yes,' Fanny nodded. 'It takes all tastes, doesn't it?' She closed the door, almost, Charmian thought, as if she was frightened the pair would get out. Without adjusting their clothes.
The house was so arranged, she soon realized, that the erotic heat was raised with each floor level.
The top-floor room was a bedroom furnished in heavy Victorian style. A woman lay on the bed; she appeared to be in the process of undressing, her legs wide spread; across the room stood another woman,

bare breasted. A male figure sat on a chair. Or did he sit? There was something fixed and unpleasing in his posture. He was about to move. He wore a striped shirt, and a stiff white collar, but naught else. His bodily equipment was not left to the imagination.

'My, my,' said Charmian. 'Interesting suggestions here . . . saleable, I should think.'

'Oh, shut up.' Fanny turned away. 'You don't know what you're talking about, it's worse than you think.'

Charmian savoured her anger, wondering what lay behind it. Fanny was not usually so sharp with her. 'Is this the lot?'

'There's an attic,' said Fanny. 'I haven't been up there.'

Charmian said: 'You could call all this a museum piece.'

'She's moved,' said Fanny, 'that one on the bed. Her legs weren't like that the first time I looked.'

'You may have disturbed things . . . I daresay the limbs are jointed.' For use, she thought. These mannekins had not played an entirely passive part in love games. 'I should think they are valuable.' There would certainly be a market if you knew where to look. Fanny need not despair of a profit.

There was no enthusiasm in Fanny's voice. 'They move, you see. Move about the house, for all I know. Something's got into them.' She closed the bedroom door very carefully – there was no lock – then began to descend the stairs.

Or into you, Charmian thought. She let Fanny lead her down the stairs.

THE WOMAN WHO WAS NOT THERE

At the front door she said: 'Why did you bring me here?'

'To show you. To tell you they moved. Do you believe it?'

Charmian said in a level voice. 'No.'

Fanny opened the front door, let Charmian pass through it, then locked it behind them. 'All right. Fair enough. But I told you.'

Out in the street, the rain falling on the cobbles, Charmian asked her where she was going now. 'Can I give you a lift? I have the car not so far away.'

Fanny considered, 'I shall go to the club; I'll walk thank you, it's not far. I need the air.'

The club was for the elderly residents of inner Windsor. Fanny had three close friends, all women whom she met there regularly.

'Right.' Charmian kissed Fanny gently on the cheek. Something was puzzling her, over and above Fanny's remark about the wax figures moving, but she could not put a finger on it. 'Look after yourself. And sell the place; I would.'

Fanny watched Charmian walk away.

The local police must have known about the wax figures and the nature of them; the police always knew about that sort of thing. Charmian wondered whom she could ask for information about that strange house. Her colleague Dolly Barstow who worked with her on SRADIC, always well informed, was too young to know much, if she had heard of it at all. She needed an old-timer.

She considered who there was: Superintendent Horris was old enough but had only recently come into the Windsor area. George Rewley had sharp antennae but was on the young side. Then she remembered Inspector Frank Felyx, just retired, and whose father had served in the district before him. It was said he remembered all that there was to remember.

As soon as time allowed on the next day she made her enquiries and was told that she could often find him at his local, the Holly Bush on the Merrywick Road. Or, if she chose her time, then he would be in the police canteen in Crown Street. He was a man of regular habits.

Eventually she found him in the Crown Imperial, in Empire Street, so he was not as regular in his habits after all. The pub was a quiet, cosy establishment with a snug parlour full of dark oak which looked unchanged since Victoria had sat on the throne. Charmian could understand why Frank had transferred his patronage. He was on his own, sitting in a quiet corner by the fire. He was surprised to see her, but polite.

'You've given up the Holly Bush, then?' Her question let him know that she had been looking for him, but he would guess that anyway.

'A new landlord, ma'am,' he said placidly, 'and I'm not quite sure of him yet, so I'm giving the Holly Bush a rest while I make up my mind.'

'It has changed a bit,' Charmian had thought it had a splash of glitter that not everyone would like, as well as loud music.

'What will you drink, ma'am?'

'No, Frank, let me order.'

THE WOMAN WHO WAS NOT THERE

'Right, ma'am. Thank you, I won't say no.'

He was amenable; she had been his superior officer, a well known figure with whom he had once worked some years ago on a child abuse case and had come to admire. He did not claim to know Charmian well, nor did he wish to – he found her formidable – but he knew her husband because his grandfather had been butler in Sir Humphrey's grandfather's country place, and although those days were over they still counted for something. Sir Humphrey Kent was gentry and although Charmian was not by birth she had married into it. Class had rubbed off on her. In Frank's eyes, anyway.

But mostly he respected her because she was a very good officer and he knew her track record. So he was polite, friendly, but in no way humble; that was not how it worked.

She came back from the bar with beer for him and dry sherry for herself.

Charmian, not really understanding all these nuances, was just friendly and professional to a man she liked.

He wanted to tell her about the latest local scandal involving two doctors and a horse, but was willing to be diverted to the house in Leopold Walk.

'Oh yes, we knew all about that. I knew more than most because you could say I inherited what I know from my dad. Everyone knew about the place, or everyone who wanted to; I wouldn't say the average church-goer knew, but of course the police did. Not that it caused any trouble – kept very private and quiet so there was never any cause to go in. Waxy House, it's called by those who want to give it a name. Or just Number One.'

He drank his beer.

'Of course, it wouldn't rate anything now, and not everyone fancied playing with the dolls then. Although Dad said what those dolls could do was masterly.' He looked thoughtful. 'I think I've got the wrong sex there, but you know what I mean.'

'Who owned it?'

'A Mrs Matilda something or other... Can't remember, but she died just after the war and Waxy House hadn't been operating, if you get me, for years before that. I think people did go in sometimes for old times' sake, more of a museum, like. The taste for it had died, I suppose, although Dad said it had its regulars to the end. Only not many of them.'

'I don't suppose there were ever very many of them,' said Charmian. It must be a specialized taste, games with dolls, even highly sexually organized ones. 'I don't suppose there were ever any women clients?'

Frank looked shocked, or tried to; he was in fact unshockable. 'No, ma'am, not that I heard. Although what Mrs Matilda got up to in her spare time might be worth thinking about.' He grinned. 'But the neighbours never complained... There were neighbours then; now the other houses are just little businesses of one sort of another and anything could go on and they wouldn't care. Not that it does as far as I know.'

'Closed down and full of dust.'

'You've been inside?'

Charmian nodded, without enlightening him further.

'I haven't thought about it for years,' he admitted. 'And if I did, then I suppose I thought it had been turned into something else... I always thought that the old lady never really owned it, just kept it, and that the real owner was some old queer in London. Or elsewhere,' he added generously, willing to spread the blame.

And you made a good guess, Charmian thought, remembering how Fanny had received her inheritance. 'Not in Windsor?' she probed.

'No, we'd have got to know,' he said simply.

Charmian nodded, understanding.

'Nor Cheasey?' she suggested. 'They go in for practically anything there, don't they?' Cheasey was the area beyond Merrywick and Eton, where crime was part of the way of life. Nothing grand, just endemic. Cheasey men were famous for it.

Frank was clear on that idea. 'Not their style... It's straight up and down and no frills there.' He gave a chuckle; the drink and the gossip were relaxing him, and he let a little hint of the bawdy creep in. 'They can be wicked enough, as you and I know, but not fancy. No, Waxy House wouldn't do for Cheasey. Each place has its own taste in sin, you know.'

Charmian knew what he meant. In her career, she had worked in the Midlands, London and now here in Berkshire, and she had come into contact with all varieties of sin. There were tastes in sinning which seemed to be geographical. More of one thing in the north, more of another in the south. It was interesting, she thought, that both of them, experienced in all manner of ill-doings, could still use the word sin.

Sophistication did not wipe out the concept, after all, but only served to strengthen it. You still believed in evil as well as crime.

Frank looked towards her, wondering if at last she was going to tell him what this was all about. He was well aware that he had been pumped – he was experienced in the process, was known as the memory man with a fund of anecdotes. He had always played with the idea that when he retired he would say: No, sorry, can't let you have that story, I've sold my memoirs to the *News of the World.*

He finished his drink. 'May I get you one now, ma'am?' he asked.

Charmian declined. 'No, I'd better be on my way, but thanks. You've helped.' She hesitated, then said: 'The house has been inherited by an old lady I know, that's why I'm interested.'

His eyebrows went up. 'Some inheritance. I hopes she knows what she's got.'

'She's finding out.'

'Mind you, if she ran it as a museum it would be a money-spinner with the tourists . . . If the town would let her do it, that is; not quite the Kings and Queens of England, is it?'

'Did you ever hear any other stories about it? Apart from the sex games? Was it ever said to be haunted?'

'I am sure it is, ma'am, but not with anything you and I would see, just something of the smell of it, I should think. Houses that get used that way never quite throw off the smell, I don't think. Not that I'm an expert.'

Charmian wondered what the other inhabitants of

Leopold Walk made of it. They must be an oblivious bunch, she thought.

'Who else is there in the Walk?'

'All business places, only there between nine in the morning and six in the evening. Number four is Bacon, Accountants, number three is C. and C. Architects, and number two is a Computer Wizard.' He had it all summed up.

'And you tell me none of them notice Waxy House?'

'Oh... ah... maybe.' He grinned at Charmian. 'Look at it as they pass, I daresay, think what a dirty neglected house, wonder who owns it, and move on.'

What his comment told Charmian was that he himself had watched Waxy House over the years, and continued to do so. Interesting, she thought.

He continued with his survey of the inhabitants of the road. 'Number four: Bacon, Accountants, a smallish firm as you'd expect, the boss Bertie Bacon, and a couple of other workers and a junior, nice kid with curly hair, Angela Bishop.' He grinned. 'Well, she's my granddaughter, so of course I like her. Number three, Mr and Mrs Fenwick... Chose the name from their Christian names, I suppose. Just them, run the firm alone. Designing a new church, I've heard. Got a big cross in his workroom, I guess for inspiration. Mrs is a beauty. Strange sense of humour. Blackish.' He laughed. 'My joke. Number two: the computer chap, Harry Aden.' He rubbed his chin. 'I call him Daddy Christmas.'

'Oh? Why?'

'He's got a round, chubby face... And he was Father Christmas at a charity show I was on duty at.

He likes kids, I suppose. That's him, then. The gossip was he fell for Mrs Fenwick, but I don't know about that.'

Charmian got the fleeting impression that he did not really like Daddy Christmas.

'The real owner of number one did live in London,' she said, 'in the West End, or so I've been told.'

'Yes, never saw him myself but my father said he was a gentleman of the old school and he had inherited the house himself and didn't know what to do with it, but I don't know about that . . . William Beckinhale, that was his name.'

I was right to come to you, decided Charmian quietly. You know all there is to know. May not be much, but what there is you've got it.

'Have you looked in the window from the street?' she asked, sure that he must have done.

'Too dusty to see much.'

Charmian nodded. 'The dust of years, I suppose.' Still, she and Fanny had managed to see through the windows.

'So it is . . . One odd thing, might be my imagination . . . The windows seem a bit cleaner than they did. Not clean, I wouldn't say that for a minute. No, but last time I passed . . .' He hesitated. 'Not that I do often, you understand?'

'Of course,' said Charmian, helping him out. She thought he was more interested in Waxy House than he was admitting. 'Of course not. But when you did last?'

'I thought that ground-floor window, the one that gives straight on to the street, and the little panel of glass in the door... They seem cleaner. Strange, isn't it?'

'Yes, it is.' Possibly Fanny had cleaned them – unlikely, but it might be worth asking. But if she was asked, would she not start to wonder whether one of the wax ladies had risen to do a little cleaning? Charmian might laugh at the idea but Fanny probably would not.

Frank gave her a sharp look. 'Perhaps your friend has done a bit of cleaning?' He had read her thoughts.

'I don't believe so; she doesn't like being in the house on her own.'

'Is that so'

'Could anyone get into the house?'

'If they wanted to, Leopold Walk is dead quiet late afternoon and weekends... Any sign of a break-in?'

Charmian shook her head. 'None that I noticed. But we didn't look.'

Frank left it there, but she guessed he was wondering at her interest. They parted quietly, Frank going back to his drink.

'Goodbye, m'lady,' he said as she left, revealing in his own way that he knew she was now Lady Kent and that, off duty, he liked to call her that.

I don't know if I did much good there, Charmian thought as she got into her car, except to amuse Frank. But he certainly has had his eye on Waxy House and that's of interest in itself, because Frank is known to be a man who does not waste his energy. She had the strong impression that he knew more about Leopold Walk and Waxy House than he was saying.

She wondered how personal was his knowledge of

Waxy House. No, surely not. She accelerated and drove on smartly, allowing herself a small giggle at the idea of Frank disporting himself among the ladies of wax. Was he married? She had an idea that he was a widower. Easy to find out, but really no business of hers.

At the moment no business of hers, but it might be one day. That was the thing about being the boss of SRADIC; you never knew what you might be obliged to take notice of.

She drove back to her office, feeling guilty (a guilt she was sure Frank did not share), like a child who had skipped a lesson.

It was after six when she arrived. Everyone else had gone; her junior assistants Amos Elliot and Jane Gibson had departed, leaving tidy desks. Inspector Dolly Barstow had gone from the small alcove which was her private area, not so tidy there, and George Rewley, who came and went, had come and gone leaving no sign of his presence. Except that there would probably be a pile of notes from him for her to read and inwardly digest.

She pushed open the door to her office, and, yes, there on her desk was a blue folder with a scribbled note on it in Rewley's writing.

She had made her room attractive with bookshelves lining the walls and a handsome antique desk that had been her present to herself when she got the position as head of SRADIC. The room looked scholarly, though she was not a scholar; she had a good degree from a Scottish university and another from an English university, but she liked to be out in the world taking action, stirring things, asking questions and getting answers. And then she needed this quiet room to withdraw to, somewhere to do her thinking.

A scholar she might not be, but a thinking woman she was. You could not do the job she did, which was essentially one of analysis and resolution of puzzles, using the sceptical mind, without being a thinker.

At the moment, they had on board (and the simile was not inapt – they were a kind of ship) a probing into a suspected fraud, a suicide in Cheasey which might be murder, and possible arson in Merrywick.

She threw her coat over the chair and read the note that Rewley had left her. Although she would never admit it, she found Rewley an attractive but intimidating man. The only hearing member of his family, he could lipread. More, he seemed to read minds.

'This was murder,' his scribbled note said of the Cheasey death. 'We must work on it.' An Irishman had come into Cheasey to work and had been killed. Thrown himself in front of a train, a self-killing the verdict had been, but Rewley thought otherwise. Not political, he said, no IRA connection (it wouldn't be in Cheasey, Charmian thought, they never even used their votes), but hate. Yes, that was Cheasey, hate. Hate especially for outsiders. Cheasey men did not like foreigners.

Charmian put the folder aside, to be studied later. She trusted Rewley's judgement. The reopening of the case would not be done by SRADIC; it would go back to the original investigating team. She looked in the folder. Oh yes, Inspector Paul Perfect had headed the team; a nice man, and a hard worker, but not one to see far into the wood.

She was glad that Rewley was back on form. He had had a tough year since losing his young wife Kate in childbirth. As Kate had been Charmian's much-loved god-daughter she had shared his pain. The baby, a daughter, was in the care of her wealthy grandmother, who was providing two nannies and a nursery suite together with much possessive love. Rewley would have to fight to claim his child. Anny Cooper was both rich and an internationally successful artist, which made her formidable. She was also an old college friend of Charmian, who was perhaps the only one who knew how much softness and affection there was inside Anny. Certainly Anny's husband Jack did not always see that side of her, but he had his own ways of making life tolerable, times in which he disappeared and did who knows what?

Rewley had sophisticated, intellectual tastes: he read poetry, was interested in philosophy, and had, of all things for a policeman, a degree in mathematics. He would go right to the top, she had no doubt.

As Charmian finished her work and made her desk tidy for the next day, she found herself deciding to have a talk with Rewley on the subject of wax figures that moved.

Had he heard of such? Could it happen and how? A mechanism inside each doll, perhaps. That would certainly have given Edwardian perverts a thrill.

She corrected herself: *might* have done, you don't know what went on in Waxy House.

On an impulse she called him at home. 'Rewley? Tell me, do you know anything about waxworks that move?'

Rewley was cautious: 'Is this something occult?'
'I don't know . . . It may be something purely mechanical.'
'Well . . . I believe in nineteenth-century Germany they were making figures that moved. Dresden, I believe, was the city . . . Always a great place for such objects as well as fine porcelain.'
'They may have china faces,' said Charmian, wishing she had been more observant. Each figure had a pretty face; she'd assumed that face and body both were indeed of wax.
'They?' enquired Rewley.
'There's more than one figure.'
He was amused. 'And you don't know what these figures are made of?'
'Faces and possibly hands may be of porcelain.'
'What is this place?'
'Have you ever heard of Waxy House?'
On a long, thoughtful note, he said: 'No.'
'I'll tell you what I know myself.' She did so, in as few words as possible.
He listened. 'Go on . . . They sound erotic, these creatures, waxen or china as maybe. And your friend thinks they move? I think she has a vivid imagination.'
'Mmm. I believe she's beginning to think they have a kind of life.'
'Becoming human?'
'Something like that.'
'Or the dead returning to life?'
'You're laughing,' said Charmian suspiciously.
'No, not me. Or maybe she thinks the figures stepped out of another dimension . . . The Fourth, I believe

it was – capital letter, please. There was a lot of talk about it at one time . . . about sixty years ago,' he added. 'Gone out of fashion now. It was a thing of the thirties.'

'I can't believe Fanny has heard of the Fourth Dimension.'

'Fanny, did you say?'

'Yes, Fanny Fanfairly. Do you know her?'

'Of course I know Fanny. Who doesn't? Not professionally, I may add,' he said hastily. 'She hasn't been in the game for years. Except, I believe, there were always a few old admirers for whom it was Fanny, Fanny and no one else.'

'So I've been told. Well, it is an old admirer who has bequeathed Waxy House to her. He must have been in the same sort of business as she was, or his father or grandfather were, judging by what I've seen. A real old curiosity house. Well, the pursuit of pleasure has many ways is all I can say. If the figures move, never mind how, Fanny will know. She tells me she keeps an eye on the house.'

Rewley said, so quietly that she had to strain to hear him, 'I wonder if you're getting the implications?'

Charmian said: 'You mean that someone is out to get the house from Fanny . . . to frighten her away?'

'You're still not getting it all.'

'What do you mean?'

'Whoever, sex and number unknown, may be out to get Fanny.'

Chapter Two

Friday

Although Fanny relied on Charmian in what she called grandly 'my legal matters', she had a group of intimates with whom she shared emotional problems. These were three ladies roughly the same age as Fanny herself, with varying backgrounds. Ethel and Paulina Avon, sisters-in-law as well as friends, shared a small house in Windsor, while Dorie Devon, a retired actress, had a flat nearby. Ethel and Paulina supplemented small pensions by working as a high-quality housekeeping team. Dorie still did some radio work, as well as reading for audio books. When work was short and she felt impoverished, she joined Ethel and Paulina in household cleaning, where she specialized in refreshing (her word) carpets and curtains.

Of all four friends, only Paulina had married, but between them the group had a wide range of sexual experience, a subject on which they had few, if any, inhibitions. Dorie always denied any lesbian leanings but the verdict among the group was that 'if pushed, she wouldn't say no'. And, as Paulina sagely commented, when on tour and all the men were the 'other way', who could blame her?

To their liberated views, Fanny had been just

another businesswoman, albeit in a rather specialized field. 'But a field that was often the only one open to women historically,' said Paulina, the intellectual of the group.

It's a battle, they agreed, but one they were well equipped to fight. None of them was rich, and only Fanny had inherited anything, but they enjoyed life.

Another thing they had in common was that they took a great and varied interest in drink. Starting with tea and working upwards. Drink gave release, they had long since decided, and if they didn't deserve release and relief at their age, then when would they? Drugs of any sort except aspirin, however, were out. If you couldn't sleep you took a drink of tea or gin or whisky or whatever you had handy and stayed awake: it could be a pleasure.

They met each day but at no set time and no regular place. Fanny would drop in on Ethel and Paulina or those two would call on Fanny, and Dorie would hear it on the wind and call in too.

Today they were in Dorie's flat because she was decorating her bathroom with pale pink paper with golden stars on it. She didn't want help, she preferred to do it all herself, but she did like conversation while she worked.

She had laid in a bottle of nice white wine, not too sweet, and got to work. Ethel and Paulina had arrived, but Fanny had not yet turned up.

'Help yourself to wine, and pour me a glass ... Thanks,' she said from the top of her ladder. 'Now, what do we do about this business of Fan's ... Damn these stars, I can't get them level.' She wobbled backwards dangerously as she stared at the wall.

'I don't think they're meant to be level. More casual, like.' Ethel steadied the ladder. 'Like the sky.'

'I prefer them regular,' said Dorie. 'I'm worried about Fanny, there's a problem there. I mean, what is it she's saying about this house? She can't really believe those figures are moving around on their own.'

'Think she does,' said Paulina. 'Sounds like it to me. Mad, of course, couldn't happen.' Paulina was always very down to earth.

'Fan is not dotty.' Ethel was firm. 'I won't have it. Not a word of it. She's as sane as you and me. Saner, probably. With the life she's led she would have gone mad long ago if it was in her. No, if she says she thinks those dollies move, then they do.'

'Have you seen them, by the way?' Dorie stepped down from the ladder.

'No, not me.'

'Nor me,' said Paulina, 'but she did promise me a visit. I'm quite keen, actually.'

'You would be.' Dorie poured herself some more wine. 'You've always been the adventurous one.'

'Hark who's talking.'

'Fan doesn't take possession yet,' said Ethel. 'She has to wait for probate on the will.'

'She's got a key, though, and she took that Charmian Daniels round.'

There was silence in the room. They did not know what to make of Charmian, a policewoman, after all. Kind, they had heard, clever. Married into the gentry. It was a perplexing picture.

'I went to take a look myself,' said Ethel, suddenly. The other two rounded on her. 'You did?'

'Yes. What's more, I've been again. Twice. And I'll tell you this, I don't know if the dolly girls move, but if they do one of them cleaned the windows.' She had their attention and she knew it. 'The first time... couldn't see a thing, dirty, dusty windows. But the next time, I could see in. Not a lot but enough to see a kind of dining room with a figure seated in it.'

'Moving?'

'Not moving, Dorie, dead still.'

'Why didn't you tell us?'

Ethel ignored this; she was well known to like her little secrets. 'And when I went again, yesterday, as it happens, blow me if the windows were even cleaner. I could see through the glass panel in the door, which I couldn't before. Or not much.'

'What could you see?' asked Dorie. 'Bet there wasn't much to see.'

Ethel had to admit it. 'Just the staircase.' She had noticed the carpet. 'Turkish runner down the stairs, a nice bit, good stuff in its day.'

'Long past now, I should think,' said Dorie.

'Dusty, yes, but you could bring it up... Tell you what...' she paused.

'Oh, come on,' said Dorie; she was the performer, no need for Ethel to ham it up.

'Big looking-glass at the top of the stairs... mirrors all over the house in a place like that...'

Dorie rolled her eyes. 'Get on with it, we all know you saw *Death in the House of Ill Fame* at the old Odeon when you were ten.'

'I thought I did see movement in the mirror... just a flash. I don't know. Could be imagination.'

Her friends looked at each other: it was believed that Ethel had no imagination.

'Your eyesight isn't so good,' suggested Paulina.

Ethel nodded. 'That must have been it.'

Her easy acceptance of her short sight, something she usually fiercely denied ('I can see as well as any of you'), naturally at once convinced the others that she had indeed seen something move.

Mice? No, too small. A rat? A cat might have got in, cats could get in anywhere.

There was one other possibility: better to face it straight on. 'Had you had much to drink, love?' said Paulina bluntly.

'I will not deny it, I had had a small sherry.'

'One small sherry wouldn't make you see things,' said Paulina. 'Not you, Ethel, you've got a stronger head than most.'

They looked at each other and there was a moment of silence. A wordless consensus was arrived at.

Dorie summed up: 'We'll have to leave it open.' She grinned at her friends. They were enjoying every minute of it. She pushed the ladder further into the bathroom, so that she could join her friends by the fire.

'Let's open another bottle,' she said joyfully, 'and I picked up some smoked salmon sandwiches from my grocer to eat with it.'

Her grocer was a grand emporium in Piccadilly which she used only when in funds, but she had done a TV advertisement this month and was rich. Relatively speaking. Well, richer than the month before, she explained, which money also accounted for the excellent quality of the wine she was opening.

'Let's mull it all over.'

Dorie's sitting room was small but cosy. She liked warmth and flowers and soft bright colours on the furniture and floor; she had chosen an apricot pink and had managed to match her lipstick and nail varnish to it.

Ethel and Paulina came from a more spartan house in which oak furniture and dark curtains made strong notes, but when you were in it with them it felt homely and used. Also, they were better cooks than Dorie or Fanny (who could not cook at all, her life had never been domestic), so it was a comfortable gathering when the quartet met in the Avons' house in Mountbatten Road. Fanny's establishment was the least comfortable of all, just a couple of rented rooms, but these were so full of the interesting mementoes of her life that there was never a dull moment there. She had a good nose for wine, too.

Dorie looked round. 'Where's Fanny? She's usually here before this.'

'Yes, she's not a late one,' said Ethel. 'First to come and last to go, as a rule. Habit, I suppose.'

'Perhaps the dolly girl has got her.' Paulina was half flippant, half serious. Into the silence that followed her remark, she said: 'Well, we haven't been taking it seriously, have we? There might be a threat to Fan, there. You know, something hidden, dark.' She closed her eyes. 'I can feel it, I think, I sense it.'

'Oh, shut up, you,' said Ethel. 'You're no more psychic than I am.'

'You're one to talk, you that saw things...'

'A thing, a movement, maybe I saw it and maybe I didn't.'

Dorie went to the window to stare down at the street. A lamp illuminated a stretch of pavement but there was no sign of Fanny. The street was empty.

She turned to Ethel. 'Do you think she's gone to your place? Or the club? She might have forgotten. She's been vague lately.'

'No.' Ethel was clear about it. 'Saw her in Marks... we spoke, she knew it was here, she said so. Besides, we're not far away, not much of a walk, and she's a great walker. If she didn't get an answer, then she'd come on round.'

'So she would,' Dorie nodded.

'She trusts too much in her friend, Charmian Daniels,' said Ethel, suddenly. 'She told me over the frozen fish counter. I say friend, a dangerous friend, I would call her... Keep well clear of the police in any shape or form, I say. Still, it shows that Fanny is worried.'

'We know that already,' said Dorie, 'and we're worried too, or what is all this about?'

Paulina had her own point to make. 'I met Charmian Daniels myself, Lady Kent she is really. Cleaned her house. Pretty little house, bit neglected, nice furniture, though, and a dear little cat. I liked that cat. You were there, Ethel.'

'I remember,' said Ethel.

'Did Fanny say what her police friend thought about Waxy House?'

'She was interested but she didn't say much. Not a lot of help, Fanny thought.'

Paulina found her voice again. 'Charmian Daniels is a good-looking woman, dresses well.'

'Oh, you're obsessed with looks,' said Ethel; there were occasions when she found her sister-in-law irritating. 'Stick to the subject: we're worried about Fanny. And where is she?'

Dorie got up; she had heard a noise. She went to the window again. 'There's a taxi stopping . . .'

The others joined her at the window. 'That's Fanny getting out,' said Ethel, surprise in her voice.

They never took cabs; years of living economically had left their trace. You only took a cab if you were ill. Otherwise it was the bus or you walked. It was true that Dorie occasionally took a taxi when working, but that counted as justified expenditure.

'There's something wrong,' said Dorie in a decided voice. She went towards the front door and the others followed her. She opened it and they waited as Fanny laboured up the stairs. They could hear her slow steps.

She came up the last flight of stairs, and saw them. She held out her hand as if she needed help. Then she staggered, sinking down on the stair.

Dorie hurried forward, put her arms round Fanny and helped her into the flat, as the other two clustered around, leaning forward, making anxious noises. Fanny was pale, her hair untidy. She leaned against Dorie, looking at the other two.

They saw the horror in her eyes.

Dorie brought some brandy, Paulina went to make some tea, and Ethel pushed Fanny into an armchair.

'Don't talk till you feel better. No, don't talk, just wait.'

But Fanny did talk.

With her hand gripping her glass of brandy, she let the words come ripping out as if she couldn't stop them.

'I went to look at the house. I've been going often, once or twice I've gone in, other times I just look in the window . . . You can see through now. Been cleaned to frighten me.'

'I know,' said Ethel. It seemed likely to her. Nasty.

Fanny took no notice. 'I usually go around six in the evening, the time I walk the dog.'

'You haven't got a dog.'

'Be quiet, Ethel,' said Dorie. She steadied Fanny's hand, which was shaking, spilling the brandy on to her skirt. 'Let Fanny get on with it.'

'I did have a dog, you know I did, and so it got to be the time I took a walk. I was regular. It's my house but I don't have possession yet until the will is proved . . . Possession,' she said, her voice husky. 'She's got possession, she's the one in possession.'

Dorie put her arm round Fanny. 'What are you talking about, Fanny?'

'I was looking through the glass in the door. I saw her walking down the stairs . . .'

'Who, Fanny? Who did you see?'

Fanny drank some brandy. The colour was returning to her cheeks. 'The woman from the top-floor bedroom. I knew she moved. I saw her coming down the stairs.'

She let them all see her face. 'She was wearing her nightgown . . . transparent chiffon. Diaphanous, they called it. Lucille, she was the court dressmaker, used to sell nightgowns in what she called her Rose Room then. When she, the doll, was made, that is . . . I knew she could walk. She came down the stairs towards me.'

'Did you see her walk? Someone behind pushing, surely?'

'Not move, but she stood there, another second and she would have come down the stairs.'

Dorie and the other two exchanged looks. 'So what did you do, Fanny?' she asked gently.

Fanny leaned back against the chair. 'I think I fainted, people always say that, don't they? But it was how it was. I blacked out, I suppose. The next thing I remember is crouching on the doorstep. I dragged myself to my feet, I couldn't walk at first, then I got to the end of the street . . . There's a cab rank round the corner.'

'Right, Fanny, right.' Dorie kept her voice soft, Nurse Dorie, she thought. 'Drink up the brandy. Ethel, pour us all a cup of tea. I know I could do with one.'

They drank the tea in silence, but it was a silence with questions hanging in the air.

What had Fanny seen?

Could she truly have seen anyone, anything?

'I know what we ought to do,' said Ethel. 'We ought to go round to Waxy House now, this minute, and see what's what.' She looked at Fanny. 'What about it?'

Fanny shuddered. 'I couldn't bear to.'

Dorie weighed in with her comment. 'Yes, you're right, it's what we should do. One of two things: the other is to call in Charmian Daniels.'

Fanny looked at the teapot. 'Can I have a cup of tea now? I think I'll feel better after a cuppa.'

'Of course, love. Pauly, will you pour?' Dorie moved away to get the sandwiches; tension always made her hungry, and Ethel was always hungry. How she kept so slim was a mystery. A fashion plate she was not, and Dorie always wished she could take her in hand, but no one, not even a close friend, pushed things with Ethel.

'I can't decide what to do just yet,' said Fanny. 'Let me sleep on it.'

'Want to stay with us?' Paulina handed over the first cup of tea.

'Thank you. Can I see how I feel later?'

They played bridge for the rest of the evening. Not one of them played it well but they enjoyed it. As card players, they had started with whist and graduated to bridge under the tuition of Dorie, who said it was a handy game to fill in the time when you were filming.

At the end of the evening, Fanny said: 'I'll be all right in my place tonight. I'm not alone there, after all, and they're good people. I'll speak to Charmian Daniels tomorrow. I'll telephone, I expect, or leave a message. She's a good sort, and she was interested, so she'll answer. I'll see what she says. I trust her.'

'You can,' said Ethel. 'A woman who is good to her cat is a good woman.'

'I wouldn't go so far as to say that,' said Dorie, 'but I know what you mean. All right, Fanny, let's leave it like that.'

Paulina gave a little shrug. 'I agree with Ethel,' she said. 'Why don't we all three go and have a look at Waxy House ourselves tonight.'

'No, I couldn't. I'm never going into that house again,' said Fanny.

'You may have to,' pointed out Dorie. 'You'll own it.'

'I'll sell it. I always meant to as soon as I knew. I've already been into Jenkins and Jones in Paradise Street and spoken about it. They can handle it. Anyway, probate takes about six months. I'm not going to think about it until then.'

But she knew she was. The sight of that figure coming down the stairs, breasts outlined under the soft silk, would never leave her. The face, too, gleaming and pale.

Dorie, more sensitive than she sometimes appeared, put her arms round Fanny's thin shoulders. 'Come on, lady of the night.'

'In retirement,' said Fanny, sniffing back a tear. She was both touched by her friend's kindness and frightened for herself, but she could not resist the joke.

'In retirement, of course. I'm never going to retire myself and neither will Ethel and Paulina. We three will walk you home.'

Coats were retrieved from Dorie's bedroom and the party set off. It was a fine evening, if cold, but it was not far to where Fanny had her rooms.

On the way, they crossed an ancient stone bridge that passed over a tiny stream that filtered towards the Thames. Fanny hesitated, reached into her pocket and threw a small object into the river. It glinted as it fell, making a muted splash.

She did not look at her friends. 'That was the key,' she said over her shoulder. 'Got rid of it.'

THE WOMAN WHO WAS NOT THERE

Without a word she walked on quickly, the others following in silence.

'Watch you while you go in,' said Dorie. There were lights on in the house; Fanny would not be alone. Fanny kissed each of her friends, walked up the three steps to the big white front door and turned at the top. She waved, put her key in the lock, then went in. She did not look back.

For her the night was not yet over; she had to sleep through her nightmare, but she would not say so to them. In the morning, if she lived that long, she would telephone Charmian.

The other three waited until the door closed with a thud, then they looked at each other.

'Right,' said Dorie. 'We all think the same, don't we? We're going to take a look at Waxy House.'

'Can't go in,' pointed out Ethel, with her usual decision. 'Fanny chucked the key into the water.'

'No, she didn't, I could see. It was a 10p piece she threw in, she was lying.'

Ethel accepted it with a nod. 'Fanny does tell lies,' she agreed placidly.

Paulina pursed her lips. 'Not lies, exactly. More fairy stories.'

'Think she's telling stories now?' asked Dorie. They all three had fantasy lives to some extent, it was admitted, but just a resort, something to cheer up a girl when low in spirits. Dorie thought of getting that BIG part, Paulina of her husband coming alive again, Ethel fancied a demon lover, but then she thought that, after all, perhaps a bottle of champagne would be even better.

Ethel wouldn't have it. 'No, I saw something, remember.' She led the way forward in silence, wondering exactly what she had seen and how. And why. Why was quite a question. She thought about why as she walked, head down, first of the three of them to get to Waxy House.

Some streets have no character to speak of, but Leopold Walk had a subdued character of its own, somehow giving the idea that it was a street that knew how to keep its secrets. There was a quietness to it; no lights shone, and even the cobblestones drank in the light from the street lamps rather than reflecting it. As it happened, the lamp at the end of the street, in front of Waxy House, was dark anyway.

The three women paused for a moment to look down the row of houses.

'Not very cheerful, is it?' commented Paulina.

Dorie agreed. 'Mostly business places, no one lives here.'

A high brick wall closed off the end of the street and abutted on to the house of Bacon, Accountants. Next door was the home of C. and C., the architects, a married couple called Fenwick, who had little to do with either of their neighbours, and had only once spoken to the owner of Computer Wizard, Harry Aden, known to Inspector Frank Felyx as Daddy Christmas, not too kindly perhaps.

'Who knows what life there is.' Ethel's face was sombre.

Paulina gave her a little push. 'Shut up, Ethel, or I'll go away. It was you that wanted to come here.'

'We all wanted to. That doesn't mean to say we like

it. I don't, I can tell you.' Ethel moved slowly towards Waxy House, which looked dark, no more lively than anywhere else in the street.

Not that it was more likeable, Dorie felt, on that account.

She gave herself a little shake. This was letting imagination get the better of you.

But she could not hide the interest she felt. She pressed forward behind Ethel. What was there about the improbable and even the impossible that fascinated the mind?

It was not easy for all three to stare through the ground-floor window to get a good look into the dining room because the gap in the heavy curtains was narrow, so they took a turn each. The darkness made it more difficult still, and Dorie, as she stepped back from her turn, reflected that she ought to have brought a torch.

She turned to the other two who had looked and remained silent. 'Couldn't make out much, could you?'

'No, indeed.' Ethel was disappointed.

'Makes you wonder what Fan saw,' said Paulina.

'You're not doubting?' Dorie faced her friend.

'No more than we all were when we started out.'

Ethel marched up to the front door, the scene at which she herself had seen something. Or nothing? The movement of a cloud on the looking-glass, the swaying of a curtain in the old window frame? 'Something happened to Fanny here,' she said stoutly, 'and don't you forget it.'

'We wouldn't be here if we didn't think that,' said Dorie, 'but reason has to come into it.'

'Oh, reason,' muttered Ethel, her nose pressed up against the glass panel of the door. She shook her head. Nothing to be seen, except a narrow stair with dusty carpet on it.

Dorie went for her look and walked away quickly with a shrug, to be followed by Paulina, who took a long, interested look. 'Very dirty,' she said, drawing away at last as she heard Ethel fidgeting. 'We ought to put in for the cleaning job here.'

Ethel pushed her friend aside and bent down to peer through the letter-box, a heavy dark object with baroque decoration. She stayed, her face sharpening.

'What is it, Ethel?' asked Dorie at last.

Ethel moved away. 'There's a smell in there. I don't like the smell.'

'Death?' Paulina was half hopeful, half fearful.

Ethel was thoughtful. 'No, not death, living, maybe . . . Something that smells.'

'What kind of smell?'

Ethel hesitated. Is it medical? Sort of. Would the word be clinical, antiseptic? No, that wouldn't do either, because there was an earthiness as well. 'Smell for yourself,' she said.

First Dorie and then Paulina put their noses to the letter box. 'Just smells like good old-fashioned damp and dust to me,' said Dorie.

There was a dampness to it, Ethel thought, but damp with a difference.

Without much more talk they parted, Ethel and Paulina to go one way and Dorie another.

The street behind them was quiet, the house silently nursing its own secretions while the living

THE WOMAN WHO WAS NOT THERE

hands that had carefully moved the wax figure down the stairs to frighten Fanny twisted and turned with a life of their own. They were hungry, active hands...

POETIC INFORMATION

A poem by Angus Cairns, aged ten. A pupil at
Abbots Langton School, Merrywick.

> By the river, willow veiled, walks a boy with eyes beguiled.
> Watching the water, gleaming, flashing.
> A skein of mallards high flying, swans and cygnets splashing.

Angus walked on, and then composed two more lines.
> Beauty on the water, rubbish on the bank,
> Tins and bottles, green and blue, a shoe, the foot there too.

I'll show this to my dad, he said to himself. He'll know what to do. Angus was a boy who knew what it was to be laughed at and he did not want to be laughed at now. He showed his poem to his father, who went with him to the river at Runnymede, that island on the Thames where King John met his fate with the angry barons of England.

Angus's father was a police surgeon and knew exactly what to do with the foot and the shoe, although he did not always know what to do with Angus.

Chapter Three

Monday next

Fanny did nothing about Waxy House for just under a week after talking to Charmian. She dreamt about it, nightmares, but she did not speak of it, even to her friends. Nor did she mention it in the club, although she went there as usual. She knew that the trio did not think her mad or hysterical or over-imaginative; indeed, they had let her know that they had inspected Waxy House for themselves and had found it unpleasant. All the same, it would not do to keep going on about it, she said to herself.

She thought that no one was talking about her story; in fact, Waxy House was in several people's minds. Charmian Daniels found herself thinking about it at intervals in a very busy week (a fraud case to be unpicked, a child abduction case, and a quarrel with her friend Anny Cooper which must be dealt with). Nor was it forgotten by George Rewley. The inspector took himself down Leopold Walk to inspect it. Dingy old house, not one he would care to live in, but it made no other impression. All the same, he thought, weird things did happen, it had to be admitted.

He walked on down the street, past the various business houses where he was observed by a young clerk in the accountant's office, who knew he was a detective because her grandfather was a copper.

The architect, Christopher Fenwick, also saw him from his work table by the window. He was a thoughtful, introspective man, who did not know Rewley but realized he was a stranger. Because it was a cul de sac few people came down Leopold Walk. Except on business, he said to himself, pencil raised above the drawing of a new housing block to be built in Bristol, so presumably this chap was on business. His wife Caroline would have known; she seemed to know everything, which sometimes came in handy in a wife and sometimes not, but she was out of the office.

Harry Aden, sitting at his winking green screen and surrounded by all the electronic equipment that he loved so dearly, caught just a glimpse of the back of Rewley as he passed his office. And only then because he had a large looking-glass placed at an angle in his window so that from his desk he could see into the street. He liked to know what was going on.

Only Angela, the junior in Bacon, Accountants, made any comment on Rewley's tour of inspection. She went back into the office and announced to the world at large: 'I think there's a policeman checking on us in Leopold Walk.'

No one, as far she observed – and afterwards she was questioned about this – no one person took any notice.

'Come away from the window, Angie dear,' said the chief clerk, Freda Langey, who demanded to be called Miss. 'I'm transcribing a very difficult-to-read set of accounts here; it seems to have more crossings-out than you'd believe, and any number of extra clauses written in Mr Bacon's own foul writing. You're blocking my light.' A bell rang on Miss Langey's desk. 'Yes, Mr Bacon, I'm coming. Angie, back to work, please, or I'll send you out to do the accounts of Parker and Piece and you know you hate that.' Parker and Piece were a small sausage factory on the outskirts of Slough. Angela disliked going there, as had other trainee accountants before her, because she said the smell stuck in her hair. She also complained that she had noticed only women were sent, which was sex discrimination. Parker and Piece were women too but that did not influence the feminist in Angela. She went back to her seat in silence.

But that evening she spoke of it to her friend Edward Underlyne, a young solicitor in the office of Mr Grange of Grange and Grange, Old Inn Street.

The two, Angela and Edward, had been fellow students at university, close friends but no more, since Edward had then been in love with a beautiful drama student and Angela had had a bit of a fling with a young lecturer. They shared a common interest in real-life crime and detective stories, and had even discussed writing one themselves. But incomes had to be earned and they had both decided to go into business and agreed to look for positions in Windsor because they liked each other's company; they shared a flat in the heart of the town.

'That's interesting,' said Edward. 'We're dealing with a house in Leopold Walk, an inheritance. But I don't suppose he was looking at that particular house.'

'I don't know about that.' Angela was thoughtful.

'I'm remembering something my grandpa said . . . He's a detective himself. He did talk about a house there.'

'Anything criminal?'

'Don't remember. I don't think so. It was one of those conversations that you aren't supposed to listen to as a kid . . . I did, of course. I knew the crack in the floor that let the noise through.'

'What a girl you must have been. I admire you. You ought to be doing law like me. Or the police force, like Grandpa.'

'I chose accountancy because I took a maths degree and I thought it would be a good career for a woman. I think I might have been wrong. Sexist lot, these accountants, not sure if they think much of women. I may go into the City. I believe I might do well there.'

'Do you think so? Don't know if the law is any better for women . . . Yes, it probably is. Mind you, I don't know if I approve of it. Wouldn't like to see a woman LCJ.'

Angela threw a cushion at him, which he caught neatly (he was a good cricketer) and popped behind him. They lived comfortably in their platonic household, but it was edging towards something stronger every day. On his side at least – he was not sure of Angela. He admired her a great deal; she was cleverer than he was – life with her was never boring. But he flattered himself she did not find him boring either.

'I hope the policeman wasn't looking at us,' said Angela. 'Mr Bacon is the soul of rectitude, or anyway he acts it. Looks it, too. I'm not sure if I like him and he certainly doesn't do me any favours, but I would call him incorruptible.'

'No one is that,' said Edward Underlyne, the cynical lawyer. 'Still, he might be, and if he isn't I'll defend you in court if you come up.'

'Thanks, but I might do better to take my chance.' She ducked as the pillow came back. 'Peace, peace, I didn't mean it. I expect the policeman was just taking the air.' She frowned. 'I dunno, though . . .'

'Let's go and look at the old house, just to see. If there is anything wrong, I'd like to know. Be a good mark for me to find out. We are handling probate here. Besides, I'd like a walk, and then we can go in to the wine bar and have a drink.'

'You're on.' Angela got up. 'Tell you what: shall we play one of our games?'

The games were pretending to be characters from one of their treasured and favourite authors.

'Right. Dame Agatha or Dorothy Sayers . . . I feel Sayerish tonight.'

'I think it's more a Michael Gilbert scene,' said Angela. 'You know, the accountant's office and you being a lawyer.'

'But we don't suspect the accountant, you said so yourself.'

'And you said we might have to. Let's talk it over as we walk. Give me a minute to put some lipstick on and get my coat.'

'Why do you need lipstick?'

'For protection,' called Angela from her bedroom.

Hope it's not from me, thought Edward, as he shrugged himself into his coat.

Edward knew Leopold Walk since he had called for Angela from work once or twice on the way to a concert or the theatre. They walked in companionable silence until Angela stopped suddenly on the corner of the street. 'I've remembered that my grandfather called the house Waxy House.'

'Why? Do you know?'

'Wax dolls, I think. Yes, that was it, it has a collection of wax images.' She chose the word carefully because she thought her grandfather had used the word doll in a strange voice, as if he was editing what he said.

'So it's a museum? Or a small waxwork show. I remember going to one in Rome once, old and out of date, it was, with figures of Mussolini and Hitler... Interesting, though, as a relic.'

'I don't think it's like that,' said Angela in a thoughtful voice.

Edward looked in through the downstairs window. 'Can't see much... a dining table, someone sitting there. Female in a long dress.'

'Waxwork?'

'Could be. Not moving.'

'Look through the door. Is there anyone sitting on the stairs?'

'What a question.'

'I'm psychic.' She had seen bare, white knees, legs that stopped at the ankle. Where were the feet? Quite a vision but just imagination.

He looked, getting as close to the window as he could. 'There's no one there. *Personne*'.

Then he drew back. 'You know it's not a Michael Gilbert show... not rational enough.' He considered the problem. 'Too rum, somehow. Sense of evil . . . More John Dickson Carr.'

'Get thee behind me, Dr Fell,' said Angela.

Charmian Daniels, like most in the police service, was not a great reader of detective fiction, although she had heard that it was sometimes used in police training. 'Nothing like the way it really is, too much is cut out. If you wrote it the way it was, then the readers would drop dead with boredom.' She had never thought of writing one herself, although she had been approached by one enterprising publisher.

Rewley was different. He read everything and might write anything from a thriller to the great novel of the decade. She regarded him as a prodigy and an enigma. Since the death of his wife he had become even harder to work out. But that said, he was a good detective, the best on her team. He and Dolly Barstow were two of the chosen; they might not stay with her – they were both high-flyers, so called – but while they worked on SRADIC she knew she had the best.

She did sometimes find herself wishing, though – as today, for instance, when they met to discuss the papers on the fraud case – that Rewley would loosen up. Have a love affair, dye his hair, take up yoga.

Idle thought, she said to herself. 'Some coffee?' She walked across the room to the machine, small and gleaming, in which she prepared her potent and famous brew. 'I've got a new coffee blend. Guatemalan. Very powerful.' She fancied Rewley blenched, which pleased her.

She came back with a black brew. 'This report is most slovenly prepared and put together. The whole matter must be unpicked and redone . . . We need a meticulous pair of hands. Let's send Dolly.'

Dolly, across the table and hitherto silent, looked surprised. 'Not my sort of thing.'

'You'll do it beautifully.'

Dolly was silent. 'OK, you're the boss. But I have an idea we might get involved in something else quite soon.'

'Oh?' Charmian raised an eyebrow. It was for her to say what they might become involved in, not Dolly.

To her surprise, Rewley said: 'Yes, I'm with you there.' He looked at Charmian. 'It's a missing-person case: a woman came by coach, for a day trip, but didn't catch the coach back and hasn't been seen since.'

'Doesn't sound like one for us.' Charmian frowned. 'We have some supervisory authority, we check, but we don't initiate.'

What she means, Dolly thought cynically, was that SRADIC does not interfere. Didn't it, though? She could think of several cases where Charmian had certainly interfered. She was clever about finding an excuse, as a rule, and sometimes she just pulled rank.

'The case has been taken on by the local unit that works on missing people; it's very efficient. They've spoken a second time to the coach driver and to some of the passengers. The coach driver found he could remember a little about the missing passenger. He was probably lying the first time round, didn't want to get mixed up in anything, but when pressed he admitted they had chatted a bit. The woman, Alicia Ellendale was her name – probably not her real name, or that's what I've heard – this woman said she was going to have a look round the town and visit a friend.'

'So?'

'The word is going round, not confirmed because mouths are buttoned up tight, that the friend is a policeman.'

'Anyone we know?' asked Charmian. A tingle was running up and down her spine.

'A name has been mentioned. He's attached, or has been, to the Cheasey outfit.' Rewley took a breath. 'Frank Felyx. He's just retired. Done his thirty years.'

'Have they spoken to him?' Frank? she was thinking. He'd seemed relaxed and matter of fact when she had spoken to him.

Rewley shrugged. 'From what I've heard, he slammed the door in their face.'

'Really? Literally?'

'No, not literally, but wouldn't talk much, kept his lip buttoned and said he was retired.'

'What's known about this woman?'

Rewley looked at Dolly Barstow. 'Your ball, Dolly.'

Dolly was crisp: 'This is what I was told: she is a woman of about forty, probably older but doesn't look it. Medium height, bright blonde hair, almost certainly dyed. She was wearing a red suit with a lot of gold jewellery.'

'Where did this description come from?'

'The coach driver for one, and the neighbour in the block of flats in Hammersmith where she lived.'

'Anything known about her?'

Dolly looked at Rewley. Your ball this time, her face said.

Rewley spoke with his usual precision: 'The Met, who always know everything' – there was a mild irony in his voice – 'say that she ran a small but profitable stable of high-class ladies...' Rewley did not use the words 'toms' or 'tarts', which some of his colleagues mouthed so juicily, but said: 'Top-quality whores... Had been a working woman herself.'

'Wonder why she wanted to call on Frank? Pity he won't talk, that's not wise.'

'He's always had a temper,' said Dolly. 'I don't know him well, but I've noticed that.'

'How did Frank's name come in? Did she proclaim it aloud on the bus?'

'The coach driver says she named him.'

'Odd.'

Charmian looked down at her hands; a manicure would not come amiss, but she never wore rings when working. 'Blonde hair, red suit, gold jewellery. Must be plenty like that shopping in Peascod Street. Anything else? Any distinguishing marks?'

'The neighbour said she had a foot operation a year ago. She had an extra toe, and she had it cut off, but you could see where it had been. A kind of stump, apparently.'

'So we shall know her if she takes her shoes off?' Charmian was sardonic. 'I wonder what her connection with Frank is and why she trumpeted it?'

'They may have met in the way of business,' said Dolly, not without amusement.

THE WOMAN WHO WAS NOT THERE

'Yes.' Charmian accepted it. Why not, after all? 'I wonder if she knows Fanny Fanfairly?'

'Likely enough,' said Rewley. 'Anyway, we can ask Fanny. She won't shut the door in our face.'

'It isn't, as yet, anything to do with us,' Charmian reminded him. 'Anything odd strike you?'

'Yes,' said Rewley promptly. 'This is just a missing person; she's not been gone long and yet there's an enquiry. That's unusual.'

'A lot of unusual things going on at the moment,' said Charmian.

Their eyes met in contemplation of Fanny Fanfairly and Waxy House. Dolly saw the look.

'Fanny certainly knows Frank,' said Charmian.

'What is this?' asked Dolly.

'Fanny, oh Fanny, if you know our Fanny, then you know how she's given to fancies, little fantasies. She's inherited a house which she thinks is haunted. No, not exactly haunted.' Charmian frowned. 'To do her justice, it is a strange house, with wax figures in it, all women. The figures had a use. A playhouse, a private brothel. It may have been rented out, let out, or used for private parties. Out of use for years,' she went on. 'Now it's bequeathed to Fanny and she has the idea that the figures have got life in them.' Charmian stopped, pausing for breath. 'They move. Or one of them does. On the stairs, she swears she's seen it.'

Dolly shook her head. 'Is she mad? Do you take it seriously?'

'I have to . . . Oh, not the way she tells it, but I have the feeling that something is wrong in that house.

55

Or in her inheritance of it.' Charmian looked at Rewley. 'You feel the same.'

'In a way.' His voice was cautious. 'I took a look myself, inspected Leopold Walk, peered into the house. It's a dusty old place and the wax figures must make it creepy. There's a wrong feel about it all.'

'And you're not imaginative,' said Dolly mockingly.

Rewley did not answer for a moment. 'You can sense evil in a house without being imaginative.'

'And you did?'

'There's a rotten smell about it, built into it.'

'I didn't know you were such a puritan. It sounds as though it might have been quite fun in its way, not everyone's taste but not harmful, not like making use of a child, or a woman, for that matter.'

'Take my word for it,' said Rewley. 'Whatever there was of fun about that house, it's not there now.'

Across the room Charmian's fax machine was spelling out a message, but the trio turned to other business and she did not walk over to read what was coming through.

Angela telephoned Edward Underlyne that morning. He did not like being telephoned at work, and he let her know it.

'You shouldn't do this, Angie, not professional.'

'I pretended I was a client.'

'They knew you were not. Don't you think the girls on the switchboard don't know your voice?'

'I made it husky.'

Worse and worse, thought Edward. 'What is it? Why couldn't you have told me at breakfast?'

'I hadn't spoken to Grandpa then. And you didn't eat any breakfast, remember?'

'So you've phoned him? Come on, get on with it.'

'Grandpa was very strange on the telephone, wouldn't really talk. I think he may be ill . . . I'm going round at lunchtime. Will you come with me?'

Edward hesitated. 'Well . . .' He had been intending to go for a drink and a sandwich with a colleague. The colleague was a power in the firm and Edward wanted to stand well with him. Also, as Angela had pointed out, he had eaten no breakfast, and he was hungry already.

'Come on, Eddy, I went with you when your mother lost the cat because you said you needed a woman. Now I need a man. Grandpa may need man's talk.'

Eddy groaned at the prospect of discussing an old man's prostate or bladder trouble, or worse, but he liked Frank and he owed Angela. 'All right. I'll meet you in his street.'

Frank's house was not too far away from Mr Grange's office. Edward, having less far to come, was there as Angela came hurrying round the corner. Cross and hungry, still he was pleased to see her, happier for the sight. He did love her and that made him say damn inside, because love was a complication and he had no idea how she felt about him.

Now she flew at him, hugged him, and dragged him down the road. Wordlessly.

Frank's house, neat as always, was quiet. Angela

rang the bell. No one came. She rang again, this time hanging on to the bell.

Edward stood back from her, looking up at the silent windows. 'He's out.'

'No, I don't think so. I just don't think so.' She leaned down to shout through the letterbox. 'Grandpa, it's Angela.' There was a pause, then she turned to Edward. 'He's coming, I can hear.'

The door opened and Frank Felyx stood there. He was neatly dressed but his eyes were red, as if he had been crying. He looked like someone who was moving into darkness.

'Grandpa,' said Angela, moving towards him, but Frank held out his arm to stop her.

'Go away, Angela, leave me alone. I just need to be alone.'

'Grandpa—'

'No, just let me be . . .' He was already closing the door. A copper did not like being under suspicion of murder. 'Thanks, Angela, but no, no, you'll hear all about it in the end.'

The door closed. Quietly, even gently, but decisively.

Edward put his arm round Angela. 'Come on, Angie, come away.'

She was half crying. 'What does he mean? What's wrong?'

Edward walked her down the road, still holding her. 'I don't know, love, but we'll find out.'

Not good news, he thought; bad news always hurries itself, and Frank knows it.

THE WOMAN WHO WAS NOT THERE

On that same day, after her period of silence, Fanny Fanfairly had made up her mind. She knew that her trio of friends would be round to see her that morning and would want to know what she had done, if anything, about Waxy House. She knew herself to be innocent of wrongdoing, but she was a good guesser, and she smelt evil. She had thought it over and had been spurred to action by some other news from a friend in London. She knew where to go. Or so she decided: 'I'll call on Frank . . . He knows things I don't. And perhaps I know things he doesn't . . . What shall I say to him? Frank, I have news today that disturbs me.'

And that very morning, just as Dolly and Rewley were leaving, Charmian walked over to her fax machine to check the messages. Among the flow of mundane matter was one item which stopped her.

She looked across the room to where the other two were collecting their papers before they left.

'Don't go, you two, you must hear this: a shoe has been found on the riverside near Runnymede. There was a foot in the shoe, cut off at the ankle. The foot has the stub of one extra toe.'

Chapter Four

Tuesday

So that was how it was. They had Alicia's shoe with her foot in it, but no Alicia.

It was without surprise that before Tuesday morning was over Charmian was intercepted leaving a meeting by a polite message asking if she had time to talk to Superintendent Drimwade. Newly moved to the area, he was a man she did not know.

Would she come to his office?

Yes, she would, and now.

Drimwade was a tall man with very fair blond hair and a pale skin. Charmian, who liked to know who was who and what they had done, knew his career had been distinguished. He had the reputation of being clever, sharp, yet gentle. In manner, he appeared to be so, but she knew enough about life to remember that he must also be tough and ruthless underneath to have carved out the career he had done.

She was not sure she liked him, but she had learned to work with people she did not care for and whom she suspected did not like her either. Drimwade was probably such a one, but he was extremely polite.

'You can see our difficulty? Frank Felyx is a long-time serving officer with a good record, he knows everyone and has many friends. We gave him a retirement party, but now . . .' He held out his hands. 'We have to question him in what may be a murder inquiry.'

Charmian said nothing, waiting to see what he would say next.

'Let's have some lunch. I took the liberty of ordering some sandwiches and coffee to be sent along, and I can hear it arriving.' He opened the door to the corridor.

He came back carrying the tray himself, probably a characteristic piece of behaviour, Charmian thought.

'Have you tried talking to him?' she offered.

'Sent a man round, someone he knew, in a friendly kind of way . . . Frank shut the door in his face.'

'I see your problem.'

'He's not doing himself any good,' said Drimwade, pouring coffee. 'We want to keep it as friendly as we can.' He handed her a cup. 'Milk? Sugar?'

'Black, please.'

'From what I've heard, and I don't know the man well, it's not like him.'

Drimwade held out the plate of sandwiches. 'Of course, we could ask the Met for help. They're already covering the London end, naturally. They questioned the coach driver. But the light is shining on us: we've had several missing woman cases in this area over the last four years.' He looked down at his hands. 'Phyllis Adams, Jane Fish, Mary Grey and Kathleen Mace; not all were local, all were working girls although one was just a college kid working in her spare time, or the other way round, studying in her time off, but they went missing in Windsor. Names written on my heart like Mary Tudor, and the rest on files . . . I'm not saying there is a connection, probably not, but I can see why the Met are pushing this one at us.'

He shook his head. 'All in all, we really want this handled at home, kept private, but it's tricky, for the reasons I've mentioned.'

'No one wants to do it,' said Charmian bluntly. She accepted the coffee he held out to her. 'So it's my outfit that's chosen.' She did not make it a question.

Drimwade nodded, quiet. 'We would give all help.'

While keeping your own heads down, Charmian thought.

'I'll think about it,' she said.

That was not the answer he wanted and she could see he was not pleased. 'Of course, just let me know as soon as you can.'

'Oh, I'll be quick.' Like now, Charmian said to herself; she meant that SRADIC should do the investigating, but let him wait.

'One thing puzzles me . . .' she probed. 'An adult usually has to go missing for a long time without a search being made. If it ever is. But London seem to have been enquiring almost from day one.'

'They wanted her found. They weren't too explicit about their reasons, but I gathered she'd been helping them get a line on some characters they wanted to know more about: a case on the go.'

So Alicia, apart from any other profession, was a police informer. Bullied into it, probably, because of what she was.

'Is it likely she was killed because of what she knew?'

'They think not.'

Might be true, might not. Charmian said: 'You will let me have the information you have? Thanks. We'll take it on, of course.' She stood up. 'I don't have the resources for a large-scale interview-and-question survey, which might be necessary.'

'We'll give you any help we can.' He was following her to the door.

'If I want anything, I'll ask. And you'll clear it with London? I don't want any trouble there.' The Met could be very helpful, and could also be the opposite. Good relations were essential.

'I will. That's agreed.'

Charmian went back to her office to think things over. The place was empty: Amos Elliot and Jane Gibson were out, although a pile of papers on Jane's desk suggested some activity. Dolly Barstow and George Rewley were out and about also, and even Charmian's secretary was absent.

'Now where has she gone?' Charmian asked herself. A note on her desk informed her that her secretary had taken a shopping hour and would be back soon. Meanwhile, Charmian would find on her desk the latest faxes and a new report from the Home Office.

Neither Dolly nor Rewley could be reached on their mobile phones, so Charmian sent a message on each of their pagers, then settled herself down to the routine matters, but all the time her mind was ticking over on the subject of Alicia Ellendale's right foot.

What a name. It couldn't be her real one, it had to

be assumed, a working name for a working woman, you might call it. But where was the rest of her?

Dolly phoned in, and Charmian decided what she would say to her and then to Rewley.

'Dolly, I want you to come with me first thing tomorrow to see Frank; we can both talk to him. Meanwhile, go round to Superintendent Drimwade and get copies of all relevant reports, and so on.'

'What about the work I have on hand? The fire in Purely Street?'

'You'll have to keep that going too.'

Oh, thanks, boss, Dolly thought. 'Shall I get the papers for Rewley too?'

'No, he can get his own. I want him to strike up a good relationship with Superintendent Drimwade. We need it.'

'They already know each other, but I wouldn't call it a love match.'

'He'll have to do the best he can. If he fails I'll send you in to bat.'

'Great,' said Dolly, under her breath.

'Meanwhile get those reports and read them up by tomorrow. Meet me here by nine, no later.'

'Will do.' Dolly rang off muttering to herself that she had had no lunch and had meant to go out to a friend's party tonight. That now looked off.

But she liked working with Charmian, who was a good though demanding boss. Charmian had been lucky too: her career, although it had known moments of turmoil, had been upward all the time and it was Dolly's hope that a little of the luck would rub off on her. She was just coming through an unhappy love affair with a fellow officer, which had never had any future, really. Charmian had told her that it wouldn't work and it hadn't.

So now Dolly was putting her career first. She was a clever young woman with a thoughtful, interesting face that lit up into beauty when she smiled. She knew that she was a good and valued officer but in summing herself up she thought that she lacked Charmian's instinct for survival, for coming out on top.

Her colleague Rewley did not even need an instinct for survival: the gods protected him. Or so she had thought until he had lost his wife in childbirth. Dolly too mourned Kate, who had been her closest, dearest friend. The two, Dolly and Rewley, worked together in harmony with occasional moments of rivalry. Competition between them was watched with some amusement by Charmian, who occasionally made use of it to spur them on to get results. She had been that way herself.

'If you talk to Rewley,' said Charmian – and you will, she added silently – 'tell him there are ramifications in London, and I want him to find out what they are.'

When George Rewley came into the office, rather than telephoning, Charmian said much the same, except in his case he was to go off to interview the coach driver. 'South London, New Cross, I believe, is the address.'

'Don't know the district.'

'I'm sure you have a contact in the Met who does.' Or if not find one was the underlying message.

'Might know one or two,' admitted Rewley. 'One

chap I was in college with. We went through a course or two together. But I think the Met trains them not to be too friendly. Even to each other, let alone outsiders. It's their superiority complex.'

He was calm, unperturbed by being thrown into an investigation that had, as Dolly had managed to inform him by phone just a minute or two ago, 'ramifications'.

'What's the nature of the complications you think there might be?' he asked cautiously.

'Dolly told you? I wish I knew, it's one of the things I am sending you in for. But if it is in any way being covered up by the Met it must be murder plus and among their own. I don't think they blink at much else.'

Rewley looked at her to see if she was joking and decided she was not. 'The missing woman is thought to be dead?'

'She's lost a foot,' said Charmian. 'I don't suppose she gave it up willingly. I expect that the pathologists will be able to tell us if the foot was taken off a dead person or not.'

Rewley frowned. Not a nice picture. He stood up, revealing his long, thin height. But he was less thin now; he was recovering, physically at least, from Kate's death.

'How's the child?' asked Charmian.

'Very well, still under her grandparents' roof.'

Charmian nodded. It was going to be hard to prise the child away from Anny Cooper. 'It's quite a set-up Anny has got there.'

'But she's agreed I shall take over. What she doesn't

agree to is when.' He grinned at Charmian. 'But I'll get there in the end; I'm beginning to know how to manage Anny. And Jack's no trouble.'

'Jack never is. Is he still drinking?'

'On and off. Been more off lately.'

'Good.' They looked at each other. Although Charmian was Rewley's commanding officer and senior too in years, they never quite overlooked that they were man and woman. If they clashed (and this could happen), then Charmian used her sex as a weapon. Discreetly, politely and with good manners. Politically incorrect, she knew, but it worked.

'You are covering London and the coach driver, Dolly and I are going to see Frank Felyx tomorrow, early. I expect him to be awkward. Refuse to let us in, he's tried that already.'

'What will you do if he won't let you in?'

Charmian gave a short laugh. 'I won't kick the door down. I'm hoping that Dolly can persuade him, he's said to like her.'

'Probably likes you, ma'am.'

'I'm not counting on it.'

As he was leaving, she said: 'How well do you know Fanny Fanfairly?'

'Know of her more, know what she looks like. I say good morning and how are you when we meet. Not much more than that. See her around with that trio of friends. I've seen them in the theatre.' Rewley had started going to the local theatre regularly, sometimes taking Dolly, sometimes sitting alone in a front stall. 'They don't seem to mind what they see: Ibsen,

Coward, Pinter. They turn up for the lot, even for the pantomime.'

Charmian stood up. 'I'm surprised you went to a show like that yourself.'

'I took my nephew and niece.' He grinned. 'Getting in training for when I take my kid . . .'

'I think Fanny is a friend of Frank.'

Rewley nodded. 'Bound to know her, at least. Thirty years a copper, he knows almost everyone local. Everyone of interest, and Fanny is certainly interesting.'

'She hasn't lived here for ever, though, has she? Only since she retired.'

'I think she was born here, so it's coming back.'

Charmian laughed. 'I knew that. She claims she's a royal bastard, but she's never been open about who her dad was. Or her mother, for that matter. Princesses can slip too. Didn't one of George III's daughters have an illegitimate child?'

'Yes, I've heard that story,' said Rewley from the door. 'Did you believe her?'

'I'm not sure, probably not. She's a bit of an old romancer.'

'The story about Waxy House, I mean.'

'How much do you know about that? Has Fanny spoken to you about it?' To Charmian's mind that made her accounts of what she had seen at Waxy House more suspect. A storyteller likes to go on telling the story.

'Dorie Devon told me a bit. In confidence, of course. She's a pal of mine. Good actress, she still does a bit. I like women who work.'

'Dorie,' said Charmian with a frown. 'I hope she

hasn't told too many people. I think the less said the better.'

'You really are worried about it.'

'I think something unpleasant is brewing in that house. But what, I don't know. Perhaps it's just the drains. But I mean to find out. It may have something to do with Fanny or she may be the innocent victim. Fanny may be telling a tale, but she may not. There's a wrong feel about the house itself.'

Rewley said slowly: 'I think it was because Dorie was worried about her old friend that she told me.'

'Let's leave it there for now. But let me know if you hear anything else.'

Charmian was ready to leave when her husband, Humphrey, telephoned from London.

'Could you join me in London for dinner? I have to entertain a new arrival from Russia, and he's bringing his wife . . . It's important, or I wouldn't ask.'

This was a surprising invitation since the important and secretive government department for which Humphrey worked usually ignored the existence of wives. Charmian accepted this exclusion since the force for which she worked ignored husbands.

'Where?' she asked, getting down promptly to the key question.

'My club . . . We can talk there.'

'Ah.' That was the clue that told her what sort of evening it was going to be. One in which Humphrey and his new arrival withdrew into an alcove (his club was well provided with discreet alcoves where gentlemen could talk) while Charmian and the wife drank coffee. What an exciting day I'm having, she told herself: lunch with Drimwade and now dinner with a husband who only wants me there as cover. 'Do we stay the night?'

'No. Come up by train and I'll drive us back.' He hesitated. 'I need to come home to pack. The other side to this invitation is that I'll be off for a few days.'

'Over the hills and far away,' said Charmian sardonically.

'That's about it.'

'OK. I have an early start myself, as it happens.' Her visit to Frank with Dolly. 'I'll feed the animals, change into something appropriate and meet you for dinner. I can't come earlier, you'll have to manage on your own until then. I'm sure the wife is a pretty lady.'

'I hope she speaks English,' said Humphrey, as he ended the call.

Charmian was gathering her papers together when her secretary put her head round the door. 'There's a lady who wants to see you,' she said, a note of doubt in her voice.

She got no further. Fanny loomed up behind her. 'It's Fanny here. Fanny Fanfairly. I must speak to you.'

Charmian stood up. 'What is it?' Fanny had pushed into the room. 'Fanny, your face!' A long blue bruise stretched down the side of her cheek.

'I went to see Frank yesterday.'

'He did that?' Charmian took a closer look: it was a new bruise, still rimmed with red.

Fanny shook her head dismissively. 'Oh, no, no, he didn't touch me, but he pushed me back and slammed the door on me. I slipped on the pavement and hit my face on the rubbish bin outside. I can't say Frank did it.'

'It happened because of him, though,' said Charmian. 'And you think so too or you wouldn't be here now.'

'It was his expression... He's changed.' Fanny shook her head. 'I fear for him. I begin to see a terrible chain of events, of relationships.' Charmian thought that Fanny was at her most vibrant, dramatic best. But she couldn't be dismissed.

'Come on, now.' Charmian drew Fanny towards a chair. 'Sit down.' She could feel the thin old arm trembling. 'I'll give you a drink.' She was feeling for the bottle of brandy that she kept in the cupboard at the foot of her desk. 'And then you can tell me what you mean.'

But Fanny would not be stopped.

'It's Alicia and Frank. There's a story going round that a boy found a foot and that it's hers. I knew she was missing. Frank knew Alicia, and Alicia may have known old William Beckinhale left me the house in Leopold Walk.'

'You're not saying that you think Frank killed Alicia?' The word must be getting around. Didn't Superintendent Drimwade in spite of the front he put up think the same thing? Poor old Frank. Thirty years as a respected police officer and this is what you get. Hardly a vote of confidence from your friends. It was that, surely, that was distressing Frank so much, making him odd.

'Not by himself, perhaps. But who knows what he was driven to?'

'I can't see any reason for you working yourself

up, Fanny.' She eyed her old friend, who was becoming calmer; the brandy was having an effect.

'I think it may have been Alicia I saw on the stairs. I told you on the telephone. I couldn't see her feet. Perhaps they weren't there.'

'Oh, come on, Fanny.'

'I'm not saying she was there in person, but her spirit. She wants me to do something for her.' Fanny crossed herself; she was a regular attender at St Michael's. 'It's made me face up to what I must do. I'm going to spend the night in that house, to see what happens. Satan may be there.' She looked Charmian in the face. 'You don't believe in Satan the way I do.'

'Not by name, perhaps,' said Charmian. But in evil, in malignancy. In an alien force, in a dark player. She had seen enough in her work to believe in all of these things. What would her colleagues say if she stood up and said: I believe in the Devil? Take off their hats, or fall about laughing? So she turned the question aside, as she knew she must. 'Don't let's go into that now.'

Fanny finished her drink and stared hopefully at Charmian like a small dog that wants to be looked after.

'All right,' said Charmian. 'You called on Frank, he shut the door in your face—' As he had done to the police officer sent to see him, he seemed to be making a habit of it.

'He's done the same to others,' interrupted Fanny. 'Did the same to his grand-daughter; I met Angela on my way there and she told me.'

'All right, you called on him, you then fell on your face, but you don't blame Frank for that. I won't go

THE WOMAN WHO WAS NOT THERE

into what you think about Alicia. But you are now intending to spend the night in Waxy House.'

'That's it,' said Fanny, standing up and revealing she had a practical side to her and she was not trusting herself entirely to the forces of good and evil, but allowing the police their part. 'I've got my night case, and I came round here to tell you. Because if anything happens to me I want you to know where I'm going.'

Charmian picked up her coat and bag. 'Right. I'm leaving, I'll take you there.'

'Thank you. I thought you might say that. My bag's outside. Your girl wouldn't let me bring it in. I expect she thought I had a bomb in it because it looked heavy.'

'What has it got in it?'

'If I'm going to spend the night there, I want to be comfortable ... Rugs, thick dressing gown, pillow, and two Thermos flasks and some bread and cheese. Also candles and a torch.'

Also a little whisky, Charmian could guess.

Charmian picked up the case, a service clearly expected of her, since Fanny smiled and nodded as she did so. 'It's heavy. Is that all you've got in it?'

'A tape recorder and a camera. I shall stay awake and record what happens. I want proof.'

'You don't sound nervous now.'

'I am, but I mean to do it. There's a bottle of brandy in there too. And a gun.'

'Fanny! You shouldn't have told me. I shall have to take it off you.'

'Oh, it's not real, but it looks it and it makes a bang.'

'Then you think that what is happening there, if anything, has a living person behind it?'

'I'm hedging my bets,' said Fanny grimly. 'Like you, my dear, I know Satan can put on many hats, and can take in the living and the dead.'

Oh, Fanny, Fanny, thought Charmian. Then she said: 'Do you know something you're not telling me? Is it about Frank Felyx and this dead woman Alicia?' But she knew how obstinate the woman could be.

'I don't know anything, my dear, and if I choose to make any guesses, then that is my business.' Fanny got into the car, seated herself in the front and stared ahead. 'Not a nice night, dear, there's a wind getting up.'

As she started the car, Charmian said: 'I'm not sure if I ought to let you do this.' And I damn well know I ought to knock some answers out of you, and I will in time.

'I'm going to do it, my dear, and you can't stop me.'

It was not very far to Leopold Walk from Charmian's office. They were soon outside the house. Never any trouble parking here, Charmian noticed.

She helped Fanny out of the car and handed over her case. 'Thanks, dear. You go now, I'll be all right.'

Charmian watched from the car as the small figure, wearing a feather toque and several chiffon scarves with a long black velvet cloak, marched forward.

On the last few paces Fanny slowed down. At the door, she paused and turned. 'Can a house eat you up?'

'No. And if you feel like that you shouldn't stay there.'

'Oh, I'm staying.' Her gaze flicked up and down the empty street. 'All gone home.'

'Yes,' said Charmian, not knowing whether she believed it or not. 'It's quiet enough.'

She watched Fanny open the door and bang it shut behind her. The door shivered as it closed.

'You obstinate old woman,' said Charmian to herself. She sat in the car for a while, waiting to see if Fanny came out. She thought she saw the flicker of a candle light from the downstairs window.

'Well, she's got company in there,' she told herself, remembering the figures at the dining table. Perhaps Fanny would share her picnic with them; it must be a long while since they'd eaten.

The street was not so quiet as Charmian thought.

That morning, as Angela had left the flat for work (she was always half an hour or so earlier than Edward), a man had stepped forward. He was young, not much older than she was, dressed casually in jeans and a tweed jacket.

'Miss Bishop? I'm from the *Thameside News* . . .' He produced a card. 'All quite genuine, I promise you. No spoof or anything, I am exactly what I seem.' He laughed cheerfully. 'I wondered if I could have a few words from you about your grandfather, Inspector Felyx.'

Angela, who had been taken by surprise, asked why?

'Well, he's a subject of interest, Miss Bishop.' He lowered his voice, drew closer and became confidential. 'In connection with a certain missing lady and foot found by the river at Runnymede.'

Angela went white. She had heard about the foot; it had been in the newspapers that morning. She had read of the speculation about the missing woman, but she had no idea that her grandfather came into it in any way.

Angela felt herself begin to shake, but she was not in close alliance with a sprigling lawyer for nothing. 'If you want any information, then you must speak to my grandfather.' She started to walk away.

'Oh, come on, Miss Bishop. I've tried Inspector Felyx and you can guess what his reaction was: the door in my face. I'm not the only one, TV have been round, no one can get a word out of him. It doesn't look good.'

Angela pressed her lips tightly together. 'No, no,' she got out at last. 'No, no, no.'

'Well, let me at least get a photograph.' He looked up hopefully like a dog expecting a biscuit.

'No and no.' She turned round and ran back into the house.

Edward was just finishing his morning coffee while he considered the day ahead. He looked up, surprised.

'Forgotten something, love?' Their relationship had taken a decisive step forward the night before – they had finally become lovers – and the word was used fondly. When he took in the look on her face, he stood up. 'Whatever is it? What's up?'

Angela told him, her voice trembling.

'Oh, I say . . . Of course, I read about the foot . . . but I never . . .' He put his arms round her. 'We'll do something about it. Get an injunction or something.

I'll speak to your grandfather myself . . . He'll let me in.'

Angela wasn't listening. 'No, Eddy, you don't understand, you don't know my grandfather, you don't know how he is.'

Edward tilted her face towards him. 'Come on, what is this? Tell me.' He could feel her whole body shaking.

'My mother,' began Angela. Angela's mother was dead; she had died while the girl was in her last year at college. Edward had seen her through that misery – it had been the beginning of their deeper relationship. 'My mother said that although her father was always restrained and controlled because of his work he had a well of violence inside him that he did not let out often. She said she remembered that when she was a child he had an axe, very sharp and shining, that she must not touch, and when something angered him he would go out and attack a tree in the garden. There was one tree he always went to, and she said that by the time she was grown up there was nothing left on that tree but a stump.' She was crying now.

Silently, Edward calmed the girl; she submitted to drinking another cup of coffee, then she washed her face and repaired her make-up. Supported by the affectionate young man, she set off for work.

He saw her almost to the door of Bacon, Accountants, waited until she had gone in, then walked away to his own office.

When he got there he had a few quiet words with Mr Grange, whose judgement he trusted. He omitted the story of the axe and the tree.

After he had gone to his desk to get on with his

work for the day, Mr Grange scratched his head, then had a quiet word on the telephone to his old friend Bert Bacon.

'Just thought you ought to know what's blowing up. Poor girl, she might need protection.'

Bert Bacon listened to what he was told and murmured that Angela was a good girl and he would see she was looked after. In his turn, he had a conversation over a drink at lunch with his neighbour, Christopher Fenwick, the architect. He had a plate with a thick sandwich in front of him, and Christopher, tall and thin and gloomy, was eating fish and chips.

'So there it is . . . Nasty business it looks like being. I'm sorry for the girl. Harry Aden next door to you calls her the best looker around here.'

'He'd know,' said Chris Fenwick, eating three chips.

Bert, who was short and stout, looked at him with envy. 'You never put on weight and you eat all those chips.'

Chris murmured something in his defence about his wife being away.

'I don't know how you manage with her gone so much. Live out of the deep freeze, I suppose.'

Chris said that was about it. He in his turn did not need to pass on any of the news to Harry Aden, because Harry already knew it. The two men met that evening as Harry was getting into his car to drive home. He was believed to be a bachelor living with his mother, but not much was known about his private life, although he was always well informed about other people despite the fact that he was deaf and getting deafer.

THE WOMAN WHO WAS NOT THERE

Took gossip in through his skin, thought Chris Fenwick sourly. He had no love for his neighbour, although he did not show it.

Harry Aden was big all over, covered with flesh and with a lot of black hair on his arms and his face. He walked with a rolling gait and heavy tread. The earth trembled beneath him. Behemoth on foot, but a whizz at the computer.

Harry addressed himself to Chris Fenwick. 'I've got some news for you, or perhaps you know it already: the street's got a new inhabitant... The place next door to me.'

'Oh, there.'

'Yes, oh, there... We all know what it was, is still, I suppose, although it must be rotting away quietly. A kind of national monument in its way. It's been inherited... Miss Fanny Fanfairly.'

'Oh, really?'

Harry Aden gave a throaty laugh that started in his ample belly and moved upward. 'Yes, the gender queen.'

'What do you mean?'

'Ah well, her trade, don't you know. We don't have to worry about her sex.' Another laugh. 'We all know the trade she was in. Still turns a trick, I expect, when it suits her, age no barrier and all that.'

Vulgar sod, thought Chris Fenwick. 'I don't worry about sex,' he said as he got into his own car to drive home to the house he had designed for himself in Merrywick, the colour scheme of low-key white and grey.

'Oh well, right, you married men. I do, all the time, I thought we all did.'

He watched his neighbour start the car and drive away, before taking himself off to the bungalow on the edge of Cheasey where he lived with his mother, who worshipped him. He called her Mumsy and she called him Sonny. Or sometimes grizzly bear. 'Your voice would shatter glass, Mumsy,' he said to her, fondly. 'But eating people is wrong, remember that.' He slapped her broad backside. 'We have good literary authority for it.' As if I would, she had protested. 'Well, you take little nibbles,' he had answered. 'We all do at times.' And some take great big bites. Steak and kidney pie night, it would be, it was always so this day of the week.

Smashing girl, that Angela, he'd seen her. Shame if she should be in any trouble because of that dodgy old grandpa (he no more cared for Frank than Frank did for him). He'd keep an eye out for her and see if she needed cheering up.

No one cheered a girl up more than old Harry, he told himself. You stayed permanently cheered if you were lucky.

Chapter Five

That Evening

Unexpectedly Charmian enjoyed her dinner in London. It was always comfortable in her husband's club, like dining in a soft brown leather womb. Not a womb that necessarily welcomed a female form but which behaved always with impeccable good manners.

As she had foreseen, her husband and his male guest talked to each other and later withdrew to a secluded alcove in the library (where no one ever came to read as far as Charmian had seen), leaving Charmian to entertain the wife. She was called Irene and she was tall, elegant and spoke excellent English. She had opted for English with an American accent ('so attractive for a woman'), while her husband had chosen English with a faint hint of Scotland. Sensible of him, Charmian thought.

A pretty woman, blonde and *soignée*. The hair was a bleach job, Charmian decided, but well done. She wore long dark earrings and had the slender white neck to do them justice.

And she had perception. 'You are under stress,' she said. 'Tension, I can feel it. Your job, I guess, you have a bad case.'

'You know what my job is?'

She gave a little half-bow. 'Of course.' And a smile. 'You are a distinguished police officer.'

Of course. The pair had done their homework. But was it truly professional to let it show?

'Yes, a bad case.'

'Do you pray?'

'Not much.' Charmian was surprised.

'You should.' Irene was fingering a crystal drop that hung from a gold chain round her neck. Her voice was serious. 'In this case if no other. I heard a note in your voice when you said "bad". You meant it.'

Charmian said nothing, because she did not know what to say.

'It does not matter what you pray,' said Irene. 'Only that you do it. The force, the power may be there for you to use.'

'I'm surprised you should say that.'

Irene smiled. 'You thought I was an atheist because I was Russian? No, we are a deeply spiritual people.'

I'll be glad when Humphrey comes back, Charmian thought. 'Someone may be doing some praying,' she said, thinking of Fanny. Humphrey, come and rescue me.

Irene seemed to think this would be enough. She nodded her head so that the crystal moved and glittered. 'If she who prays is close to the case then that would suffice.'

'I'm not sure how close to what worries me she is, not sure of anything . . . But yes, it would be a woman.'

'She might be in some danger,' said Irene appraisingly. 'It would depend to whom she prays and how.

There are many sources of energy, from some of which she might need protection.'

Charmian's own prayers were answered because her husband soon reappeared, his conversation satisfactorily concluded judging by his expression, and the evening ended.

Charmian drove them home, her husband saying he was tired.

'So am I, exhausted.'

'You looked lovely in that dress, though.'

'It *is* good, isn't it?' Charmian looked down at the soft chiffon draped over her knees as she drove. 'Of course, chiffon is such a flatterer, especially this rich dark colour.' Although she kept her eyes firmly on the road ahead, she was pleased with the compliment, which was deserved. She was spending more on her clothes and hair than ever before, casting aside the relative austerity of her youth.

There was not much traffic on the motorway so they made good time to Windsor. On the way Charmian recounted the details of the case: the missing woman, who Alicia was . . . 'Don't know much about her yet, but I mean to find out;' the finding of the foot, the dragging into the case of Frank Felyx, now obviously in a foul temper; and then the puzzle of Waxy House.

Humphrey's eyes were closed, so perhaps he was asleep, but presently he answered. 'Take it slowly, don't get emotional, and protect yourself.'

Charmian was silent for few minutes, digesting this advice, which was more or less what Irene had said in a kind of code. 'That's not very specific,' she said, eventually.

'The best I can do,' he opened his eyes, 'and specific enough about protecting yourself.'

'You think I need to?'

'Don't you?'

This conversation is going round in circles, she thought, just like this traffic roundabout. But I know what he means and it's why Drimwade landed me with the investigation: all inquiries involving a copper whether retired or not are fraught. No one comes out of it smelling sweet, least of all the investigating officer. I knew this, and yet still I wanted to do it. Why?

Not because of any strong feeling towards Frank Felyx himself, whom I regard as an awkward, difficult man; a certain feeling for Fanny, and a definite sympathy for the missing, presumed dead, and certainly footloose, Alicia.

But mostly because it was a challenge, and I cannot resist a challenge.

She glanced down at her sleeping partner. 'Love you, friend,' she said under her breath. In her complicated relationship with Humphrey, at times like this what she valued most was his friendship. Friendship you could rely on, other aspects of a relationship were more volatile, could melt away; there one day, gone the next. But not friendship.

'I'm just going to take a look at the house in Leopold Walk . . . Check up on Fanny.'

She thought Humphrey was still asleep, then she heard him laugh. 'Wouldn't mind a look myself. I've got a faint memory of an old great-uncle of mine talking about Waxy House . . . I'm not saying he frequented it, although I wouldn't be surprised; he was up to it all right. One of those old bachelors that Edwardian England seemed to produce in quantity, with enough money to enjoy his life and not work too hard at it. He was very very old when I remember him, but lively enough in his mind even if his legs didn't work well.'

'What did he have to say?' They were approaching the turn to Leopold Walk.

'Trying to remember... Can't recall how the subject came up, something to do with the history of Windsor and Eton, I think. I was at prep school in Windsor. I must have been learning about it.'

'Did he live in Windsor?'

'Great-Uncle Palliser? Rather – grace-and-favour apartment. He used to walk every day across Eton Bridge, when he could still walk, that is. He'd been a King's Scholar, he was bright enough.'

'So what did he say?'

'More promise than performance, as far as I remember, and then he giggled... He was a great giggler, that's what I chiefly remember about him. I didn't know exactly what he meant, but I was willing to make a guess.'

'I bet.' And I was living in suburban innocence at the time. Of course, I wouldn't have been eight years old. Charmian was younger than her husband. 'Sounds as if he went there.'

'A dropper-in rather than an *habitué*, that would be Great-Uncle's style. I don't think he ever got deeply involved in anything. Or anyone. There was a story of a broken heart in his youth, but personally, I'm not so sure.'

'Poor old chap.'

'Don't believe it, he was as happy as could be. And I ought not to be rude. He left me a very desirable Poussin drawing. He did know about pictures.'

'Is that the one with writhing muscular limbs, the saint being martyred with little cupids in the background?'

'Saint Erminia. Probably she did not exist, and putti, not cupids. Putto, singular. And don't mock, it's about our most valuable possession and when we both retire we can sell it and live in comfort.'

'I notice you keep it in a dark corner in your dressing-room,' said Charmian, slowing down the car.

'That's to preserve it. Light is bad for a seventeenth-century drawing.'

They were outside Waxy House now. The street was empty but rain shone on the pavement. All was quiet. Humphrey looked out of the car window. 'Going in?'

'Not on your life.'

'It's smaller than I thought. I supposed I imagined it on a grander scale. This is a cosy little place.'

'Think so?' She laughed. 'Well, we contrived a dressing room for you out of nothing. Houses can expand amazingly if you push.'

'Well, I use the word in fun.'

There was no sign of movement, but Charmian fancied she could see a glimmer of light from an upper room which must be one of Fanny's candles. Hope she doesn't burn the house. Sitting up, wrapped in her rug, asleep but prepared to swear she never dropped off.

Charmian backed the car down the road to turn for home. 'I thought you'd want to look in the window.'

THE WOMAN WHO WAS NOT THERE

'Not me, I prefer the pleasures of the imagination...' He put his hand on her knee. 'In most things.'

Charmian laughed and drove home. It was still well before midnight.

At midnight, a group of three tiptoed round the corner into Leopold Walk. There was no need to go quietly because there was no one about, but the theatricality of it pleased them. Dorie, Ethel and Paulina had come to check on the safety of their friend Fanny. They had just finished an exciting game of dummy whist and sleep was far away; Ethel had suggested calling on Fanny in Waxy House.

'I told her it was a damn silly thing to do,' said Ethel, 'but would she take any notice? No.'

'I call it brave of her.' Dorie had wrapped herself in a thick, dark cloak. 'Especially as she's probably scared stiff. I'm glad it's stopped raining.'

'I don't think it has quite.' Paulina was never optimistic. 'It's because she'll be frightened that we've come to cheer her up. We mustn't stop, though, I don't like to leave the dog alone too long.'

'He never notices whether you're there or not.' Ethel was peering through the glass of the door, which seemed to have got dirty again.

'He does, of course he does. Dogs do.' Paulina moved up behind Ethel. 'Can you see her?'

'No.' Ethel drew back. 'Nothing to see. I suppose she's there?'

'Oh, of course, Fanny wouldn't lie to us.'

'She might have gone home. Silly fool, better if she had.'

'No, she's still there. She'd have told us.' Paulina was looking through the glass. 'You can't blame her for wanting to protect her property. It is her house.'

'That's not why she's here,' said Dorie. 'She's fascinated by what she thinks she's got there.'

Paulina looked at Dorie with inquisitive raised eyebrows. 'What?'

'The forces of darkness, spooks, possession, call it what you like. She doesn't think wax figures walk on their own, something does it for them, she wants to know what.'

'Putting her nose into things best left alone,' said Ethel. 'And I don't think it is just that, either, it goes back to the call on Frank Felyx, in my opinion.'

'But he shut the door in her face, they didn't speak,' said Paulina.

'They might have done or they might not. He could have said a few words to her all the same.'

'What about?'

'What's going on all around us? What's being talked about? The missing woman, her shoe, her foot.'

'But Waxy House and the missing woman . . . That's two different stories,' protested Paulina.

Dorie said: 'Ethel's right, she's got something. People make the connection.'

'I don't know what you're talking about.'

'I'm not sure if I do, Paulie,' said Dorie with a sigh. 'It's just what I feel.'

Ethel had put her face to the letterbox, the better to call through it. 'Fanny, Fanny,' she hissed. 'Come on, Fan, this is Ethel, your friend who wants to know if you're all right.'

She turned round. 'Dead silence, she's not answering.' She tried again. 'Fanny, Fanny...' Getting no response, she sighed. 'You try, Dorie, your voice carries better than mine does.'

'It's training,' said Dorie, stepping forward briskly. She bent down. Her voice was lower but she projected it well. 'Fannee, Fannee...'

'D'you think she's dead?' asked Paulina.

'Oh, shut up.' Ethel was stern.

'Wait a minute.' Dorie sat back on her heels, she was the most nimble of the three and could sit on her heels; training again. 'I can hear something, I think she's coming.'

'Oh, please God, it's not a wax one coming,' said Paulina, giving herself a *frisson* of delicious horror.

Through the door came a voice that was unmistakably Fanny's. Low, furious. 'Go away, mugwumps, you're spoiling everything. Hop it, push off, go away.'

Into the silence that followed, Ethel said: 'She doesn't deserve to be helped. Come on, let's leave her to it.' She took Paulina's arm and started to walk away.

'Spoiling what?' asked Dorie, as she followed. 'She's a mystery, our Fanny.'

Inside Waxy House, Fanny leaned against the wall, her breath coming fast. 'I am not frightened, I am *not* frightened. I will not be frightened.'

Early next morning Charmian drove her husband to Heathrow then she turned her car back to her own office, where she would meet Dolly for their visit to Frank Felyx. He did not know they were coming and, taken unexpected, he might be easier to interview.

She dealt rapidly with a few routine matters, then put her head round the door of the outer office to see if Dolly had arrived. Jane Gibson was perched on the edge of her desk gossiping to Amos Elliot, but she got off quickly when she saw Charmian.

'Don't worry; I'm in early. Any sign of Dolly?'

'Not yet, But Rewley must have been here before anyone because he's left a message saying he'll report to you as soon as he gets back from London.' Jane handed the slip of paper over. 'I read it; he didn't say who the message was for.' They ran things informally under Charmian's rule, and it often helped to know exactly what the other fellow was up to. 'But I don't know what he meant by the list on the back.'

Charmian turned it over. Just scribbles. 'Two Windsor addresses,' she said. The bus station and the number of a taxi rank. It was rather endearing, Rewley's economical use of scraps of paper, and also handy because it gave an insight into the workings of his mind – always useful. Might mean something, or nothing, you could never tell with Rewley, but she would remember to ask.

Dolly arrived at that moment, pink of cheek from hurrying and inclined to be apologetic. She did not explain why she was late but Charmian could guess: since Kate's death, she had moved from the flat she and Kate had once shared to a small house on the Merrywick Road where sometimes, because she was lonely and miserable, she cheered herself up with the odd bottle of wine. Or maybe a man, or both, and the mornings after were often late ones. So far it had not touched her work, but one day it might. Charmian wanted to help Dolly but so far she had not seen the way.

Sympathy could, however, take a practical form. 'There's time for a cup of coffee,' she said. 'In fact, I could do with one myself. I had to take Humphrey to catch an early flight.'

Jane slipped happily from her chair. 'I'll make it.' She looked at Amos Elliot. 'Want one?'

He was already moving towards the door. 'No, I want to get off . . . See you later.'

Dolly drank her coffee gratefully, quietly slipping an aspirin into her mouth, an operation that Charmian pretended not to notice.

'I hope he's at home,' said Dolly as they set off, Dolly driving.

'Oh, I think he will be. It's still pretty early, and he doesn't strike me as an early riser.' She did not say that she had ordered a check on Frank Felyx's movements by Drimwade's men and knew that he had not moved from the house since midday the previous day.

Felyx lived in a terrace of small but pleasant houses not far from the main shopping centre. The front garden was tidy if not beautiful, but the house itself needed repainting and the window curtains, although not dirty, looked faded, as if no one cared. Charmian had learned that Frank had been a widower for a very long while and that although he had a grand-daughter, he seemed to have no other family.

They sat for a minute or two in the car while they

discussed how to go about it. 'He likes you,' Charmian said. 'I know it's a weak and sexist approach, but with someone like Frank you have to use what you've got. You ring the bell. When you get in, I'll be right behind.'

'Or we'll both get the door slammed at us,' said Dolly, easing herself out of the car, 'which seems to be his style at the moment.'

Dolly marched up the garden path, crazy paving, so called, which she thought illustrative of Frank. She rang the bell and banged on the knocker. No point in being sensitive or coy with Frank in his present state.

He opened the door and stood there before her in an old dressing gown and striped pyjamas that looked as though they had lived and been washed through several wars.

'How are you?' asked Dolly in a polite voice.

'I'm not sick.' He looked about. No press around, thank God.

'I never said you were.'

'Just having a late breakfast.'

'Can I come in?'

He looked across to the car where Charmian still sat. 'So who's that with you? No, don't tell me, I know her.' He held the door wide. 'Well, tell her to come in; I know when I'm beat. Can't keep you two out.'

'Much as you'd like to, eh?' Dolly turned to wave to Charmian.

'You've got it.'

When Charmian came in quickly, the two women joined Frank in the kitchen. 'Want some coffee?'

'Not me. You look terrible, Frank.' Not like the man I had a drink with the other day: thinner, redder and older. 'What is it?' She studied his face. She could see traces of tears around his eyes and nose. 'You've been crying.'

'Maybe. Why not? I have plenty to cry about.'

Charmian said: 'Perhaps I will have some coffee after all.'

'I notice you don't ask why? I could say I'm mourning for myself. One day a police officer with a clean record, even if no distinguished service medals...'

'You didn't do badly,' said Dolly. 'Promotion, a commendation or two.' And a handsome leaving present with a party.

'And the next moment I'm a murder suspect,' he went on, as if she had not spoken.

'How well did you know Alicia Ellendale?... If that was her name.'

'Who says I know her?'

'She certainly knew you. Or knew of you; she had the name off pat.'

'I might have known her.'

'Was it a professional relationship?'

Frank thought about it. 'I knew her as a police officer,' he said at last.

'So she was coming to you as a professional, was she?'

'I wasn't one of her clients, if that's what you mean.'

It was what Charmian had meant. 'Did she come to you for advice, because you were a policeman? Was there some problem?'

Dolly, who had kept quiet, said: 'I bet she had a lot of problems. A working woman, not getting any younger... She might have known a criminal and been frightened. Or perhaps she had something to confess.' She looked Frank in the face. 'Or someone to accuse.'

'Now you're doing it too,' he said.

'Doing what?'

'Accusing me. I thought you were a nice girl, Dolly Barstow.'

He's just the tiniest bit drunk, Charmian told herself, and perhaps has been for days.

'So why was she coming to see you?'

'Who says she was?'

'She told the coach driver, he says so.'

Frank poured himself some coffee from the battered pot on the stove. 'And he's a reliable source, is he? Why should you believe what he says?'

'I don't know that I do, Frank, I don't know what I believe yet. I'm trying to find out. It's all speculative at the moment: all we have is a missing woman, a shoe with a foot in it and a lot of questions to answer.'

'My advice to you is to ask some more questions of that driver. I tell you that as a man who did his thirty years and got to know what stinks.'

'Do you know the driver?' asked Charmian with a frown.

'I know him, not as a friend, but we've met. Arthur Doby.'

'He's been questioned already, you must know that. And I've sent an officer of my own to question him this morning.'

Dolly reached out and drank Charmian's coffee, which had not been touched. 'Frank's got something to tell us, I think. Remember, Frank, when we worked together once, a long time ago, when I had only just been made a detective? It was that hospital job and you said I always seemed to know what you were thinking. What I thought then, Frank, was that you fancied me a bit.'

Slowly Frank smiled. 'So I did. Never did anything about it.'

'No, you were a gent, Frank . . . I know what you're thinking now. Can you trust us, that's what you're asking yourself.'

Frank stood up. The coffee seemed to have sobered him. 'I've got something to show you.'

He went out of the room, then they heard him mounting the stairs.

Charmian went to the door to listen. 'What's he doing? . . . He's not going to do anything silly, I hope?'

Dolly shook her head. 'No. Come and sit down. He'll be back.'

'Oh, you've got telepathy, have you?' Charmian returned to her seat.

'No, but I can hear. He's opened a drawer and is now coming down the stairs.'

Frank reappeared, holding a plastic carrier bag which he put on the kitchen table. He had a clean towel under his arm which he spread out, then he opened the bag and let the contents gently slide out.

A woman's high-heeled shoe.

Charmian took a tissue from her bag, which she wrapped round her right hand, then picked up the shoe. She said nothing, but looked at Frank.

'I found that shoe in the litter bin in the men's lavatory in the coach station.'

'When?'

'Nearly a week ago ... I'd heard about the missing woman, and a pal let me know I came into it ... So I went down to the coach station to ask some questions. I know some of the drivers. I found the shoe by chance.'

'I shall have to take it.'

'Do.'

'And get you in to make a statement about finding it.'

She was trying to keep her voice steady but inside she was appalled. What was he telling her?

'I'll come down, don't worry.' He sounded calmer. 'I feel better now I've told you. It's out.'

'Why didn't you hand it over at once?'

'The other shoe hadn't been found then,' he said simply. 'And there's no blood on this one. I was just guessing then ... and afterwards ...' He shrugged. 'Well, would you have rushed forward?'

'So I think that coach driver needs to be questioned.'

Outside, Dolly said to Charmian: 'Do you believe him?'

'I don't know. Not all of it, but I'm not sure which bits yet. But there's more, I feel sure. More than he's saying.'

'He's in trouble.'

'He certainly is. Tell me, Dolly, can you really read his mind?'

Dolly laughed. 'Of course not.'

Charmian looked down at the bag which Dolly now held on her lap. 'Drimwade will need to have it, and forensics will have to go over it. I imagine they'll go over Frank's house as well.'

She started the car. 'Wonder how Rewley's getting on with the coach driver. Pity he didn't know about this shoe.'

Dolly said: 'If Frank's not telling the truth, and he killed the woman, then why did he not just destroy the shoe? He didn't have to give it to us.'

'That's true. So perhaps he is telling the truth. And if the coach driver is guilty, why was one shoe in the river with the foot and the other left behind in the coach station lavatory?'

'There's no accounting for killers.'

Charmian moved her hands to start the car, then she stopped and turned her head to look again at the house. 'Wait here a minute.'

She got out of the car and went back to ring on Frank's door. After a pause, during which Charmian moved restlessly on the path, and Dolly turned the radio on in the car to play some music, Frank opened the door. 'What do you want now?'

'I want to ask you about Fanny Fanfairly. She came to see you. What did you say to her?'

'Turned her away from the door, didn't I? She slipped and fell, not my fault.'

'But she came back, didn't she?'

Frank was silent. Then he said: 'Did she now? On the watch, were you? Saw with your own eyes?'

'No. Just a good guesser.' She had struck gold, and would never admit that it had been a lucky shot, inspired by something in Fanny's manner. 'What did you say to her?'

'All right, she did come back. Wanted to talk to me again about the house in Leopold Walk. Was it haunted? Had I heard that it was? What did I think? I told her that I didn't believe in rubbish like that, and that if she wanted to find out, then she should spend a night there and see for herself.'

Charmian nodded. 'So that's why she did it.'

'She did? Silly old witch.' He seemed discomfited. 'It may be haunted for all I know; there's more than one way of haunting a house.'

Dolly looked at Charmian with curiosity as they drove away. 'Get what you wanted?'

'Just confirming a guess about Fanny Fanfairly.' And she told Dolly how Fanny had spent the night.

'Game old thing,' said Dolly, half amused, half admiring. 'But I reckon she knows how the world goes... She ought to by now.'

They drove back to the office in companionable silence with the shoe on Dolly's lap.

Charmian mused about the shoe which Frank claimed to have found. If it had been left in the coach station, then either the driver had left it or someone was trying to incriminate him. And where was the other foot? Burned, buried, or in the river? Never find it, she thought, and wondered if the shoe and the foot in the river were one of those unconscious calls for help?

As she arrived at her office, she said: 'Deliver the shoe, if you will, as I asked, and then it seems to me that your best part is to dig into the background of this woman, Alicia Ellendale. Get what help you need from

Drimwade's team – he's offered it – and let me have what you get soonest.'

Superintendent Drimwade's reception of the shoe was an icy explosion of anger that boded ill for Frank Felyx.
Charmian and he met in his office, where he sat facing her at his desk. A computer screen on his desk flashed brightly, and a fax on the shelf behind him spilled out its messages, but he ignored both. The air felt drained of oxygen.
He thanked Charmian in a tight-lipped, frozen way, and said the shoe would go at once for forensic examination. 'I'll have to talk to Felyx myself, after all,' he said.
'Of course.' What an uneasy partnership we'll make, thought Charmian with some amusement as this truth dawned on her too.
'We need to find the body, you know,' he said. 'Without that we're struggling. We can bring a charge of murder without the body but it makes everything so much harder.'
Charmian knew that too. 'She'll turn up. I'd like to know why the feet, or at any rate, one foot, has been cut off.'
'If we can work that one out,' he said ruefully, 'we'll probably know the killer. I admit it, I'm not a man of imagination and I'll want it spelled out in big letters. Why cut off one foot at the ankle and leave it by the river?' He got up and started to pace round the room. 'Oh, by the way, Cairns, the police surgeon whose son found it, said it had not been in the water long as far

as he could judge, just resting on the edge, otherwise the shoe would have come off.'

'Sounds reasonable.'

'It was just dropped there. On the edge of the river. Casual. And now we have this other shoe, if it's a match, and my guess is that it is, and it turns up casually dropped in a lavatory waste paper bin. What do we have here? Some sort of shoe fetishist? Or is the foot the important thing?' He sounded harassed.

'We only have one foot, of course. But it is the one that can be identified as Alicia Ellendale's.'

'What about the boy who found the foot and shoe? It must have been disturbing for him.'

'Yes. Angus Cairns. Skinny little lad, but as bright as could be ... I went to see him. I think he was fascinated by what he'd found, couldn't stop talking about it. I wouldn't be surprised if he wasn't having the odd nightmare. Both his parents are doctors, busy people. I know Cairns; he said he'll talk the lad through it.'

'I'd like to see him myself.'

'They live in Merrywick, give you address, he'll be at school now, of course. Good scholar, too, so I gather.'

'Which school?'

'Abbots Langton, I think.'

'A good school,' said Charmian thoughtfully. 'Better to see him at home, though.'

Drimwade let out a great sigh.

Charmian looked at him with more sympathy than she had expected to feel. This was not the sort of problem Drimwade liked to face. But he was facing it,

THE WOMAN WHO WAS NOT THERE

reluctantly forcing his mind to concentrate on it. 'Do you still believe Alicia Ellendale is dead?'

He nodded. 'I do.'

'So do I.' Charmian hesitated. 'You realize she may be in pieces? That perhaps it is not only feet at the ankle that have been cut off?'

'It had occurred to me. And of course it will make her harder to find.'

'Well, we have suspects: Frank Felyx and the coach driver.' She looked at the clock. 'Rewley is in London seeing him now.'

'Let me know how it goes; Rewley is a sharp fellow,' Drimwade said dolefully. 'I was sorry when he was seconded to you. I'll keep in touch. I was going to take a few days leave, but I won't do so now. Not just yet.'

Charmian thought with amusement: we seem to be working well enough together, after all.

But it had been a disquieting talk because of the pictures that it conjured up.

Bits of a body, is that what we're now looking for? she asked herself as she returned to her own office. And where will they be? Distributed all over Windsor? There is always the river – the body could be there. But where would the river take it?

She didn't know, although she could soon find an expert who would. It might end in divers and a full-scale underwater search.

Her mind dwelt for a time on the woman Alicia Ellendale, about whom she knew very little, who had come to Windsor for a day trip and never been seen again. She turned to the slim folder of information that had been delivered to her from Drimwade's office:

Alicia Ellendale, aged 53, although she claimed 43, real name Mrs Alicia Beeton, born Fisher, divorced. Address: 110A Greenwich Lower Road.

She ran several so-called 'Social Agencies' under different names, which had a surface respectability, but nevertheless she was up before the magistrates in Central London several times.

Now said to be retired, but is thought to carry on quietly on the side.

Height: 67 inches, approx. weight: 130 lbs. Distinguishing characteristic: the right foot had an extra toe, now removed, but the stub remains.

There was also a photograph of a plump, attractive, bold face.

Charmian sat looking at it, wondering what had happened to the woman. Had she come on business to see a client? And was Frank Felyx that client?

Or was the coach driver, Doby, a liar who had killed Alicia himself and then for reasons unknown left the shoe in the lavatory?

Funny business, that: made you wonder who was lying: the driver or Frank?

She looked out of her window where the trees blew in the wind and hoped that Rewley would get back soon. When she heard voices in the outer office she listened. No, not Rewley, a woman.

Fanny.

She got up and put her head out of the office. 'Come on in, Fanny. I can give you five minutes.' She shut the door. 'I wanted to see you, anyway. How did it go last night? I came round to see if all was quiet... It seemed to be, so I went away.'

'You must have come before the others,' said Fanny. 'Dorie, Ethel and Paulina.' She threw up her hands. 'Shouting and banging on the door... I had to send them away. It was all quiet then.'

Charmian picked up the emphasis. 'Then?' She studied Fanny's face. The bruise was fading but she looked tense and ill. 'So what happened?'

'It was quiet at first. I sat there at the top of the stairs, listening and waiting. Mind you, I had gone over the house sprinkling holy water which the good Father gave me. So, I thought, that's done you, you devils. And then the house started up.'

'Started up? What do you mean?'

'Like an orchestra, it was. First just a little noise, a creaking in the timbers.'

'Old houses do that, Fanny, as the temperature changes.'

'The house got colder too, as if a chill wind was blowing through it. And then the banging started. At first little tapping noises, then bang, bang.'

'Banging where?'

Fanny thought about it. 'It seemed all over the place... but up the stairs from the basement.'

'What's in the basement?'

'That's it. There isn't one. But it sounded like there was.' Fanny stared straight in front of her. 'And then I was frightened... I thought if I stay here one of those waxen creatures will walk down the stairs, or up, perhaps both. I felt as though there would be two and I would be caught between them.'

'That was just your imagination.'

'Yes, perhaps. I tried to tell myself that. So I wrapped myself in my rugs and curled up at the top of the stairs.'

'And? *And*, Fanny?'

'The noises died away. I think I dozed off; seems extraordinary that I could in the circumstances, but perhaps I did.' She shook her head. 'When I felt strong enough, I took my torch and looked in the room upstairs. She hadn't moved, not that one.'

Charmian looked at the old woman without speaking.

Fanny went on: 'So I went downstairs. It was beginning to be daylight, that's how I know I might have slept.' She stared at Charmian with piteous eyes: 'The dining room looked different. The cloth was still on the table, the table, all the silver and glass just as they had been. But the pair of dolls – if that's what you can call them – closer together. They hadn't moved far, just edged nearer to each other. And there was a smell of wine in the air, as if they'd been drinking.'

Charmian remained silent. She did not know what to say. What she wanted to say – that it was all Fanny's imagination – would not please her friend.

'That was what all the banging and the creaking was . . . The house was telling me.' Fanny nodded her head. 'You don't believe me, I can see that. Right, well, tell me what you make of this.'

She put her hand in her pocket and drew out a gold coin. 'A sovereign. It was on the table. Tell me who put that there? Payment, I reckon. One creature was paying the other.'

'Right,' said Charmian, standing up. 'There is one thing I can do. I'll spend tonight there myself.' She patted Fanny's thin shoulder. 'You can come or not, as you like.'

Fanny thought about it, her face drawn into deep lines around her mouth and eyes. 'I'll come,' she said eventually. 'See you there.'

Charmian watched her leave, standing by her window to see Fanny come out of the door and cross the road. So, she said to herself. If you don't believe in ghosts and ghoulies what *do* you believe, because something happened in that house.

I believe that Fanny was asleep. She had a bottle of brandy with her, she drank, she's an old lady and she fell asleep. While she slept, someone came into that house. This person left the sovereign, just to make Fanny believe in a walker from the past. That's what I believe. But why this game is being played, I do not know.

As she stood there, Rewley came in.

'I did knock...'

She swung round from the window. 'Sorry, I was far away. Well, what did you make of the driver?'

When Rewley had given his account of Arthur Doby, then she would tell him about the second shoe.

'You ought to see Doby's place... Sordid isn't in it. But cosy, somehow. He has a collection of old coins, nicely arranged, too. He belongs to a society that collects coins, part of the façade, the front he puts up... But the way he is,' Rewley threw open his hands, 'I don't know if he's a liar or not, but I think I'd want to check every word he said, and I don't think I'd ever lend him any money. Still, he sticks to what he said.' He produced a small tape. 'I took a WPC with me, and he agreed I should tape the interview as long he had a copy.'

'Play it over.'

The man had a rough, deep voice. His answers were short, never a word said more than he needed to utter.

'You didn't like him?'

Rewley shook his head. 'You ought to see him for yourself.'

'I will.' Tomorrow, she thought, after my wakeful night with Fanny. 'You should know that another shoe's turned up. Frank Felyx claims he found it in a rubbish bin in the men's lavatory at the coach station. He says it points the finger at the driver.'

'They accuse each other, then,' said Rewley. 'Which one to believe.'

'We don't have to believe either,' said Charmian. 'Give me your notes and let me have the tape.' She stood up. 'We've got to talk. I have to shop – food for the cat – but there's a coffee shop in the market. Come with me, we can talk over a coffee. I want to have your views.'

The supermarket, one of a local chain, was not crowded at that hour; she picked up a basket, tracked down the shelves where the pet food was lodged and chose a dozen tins of different flavours. Her cat liked a change of taste.

'You spoil that animal.' Rewley had picked up a jar of coffee powder and a box of teabags.

'Of course I do. It's a game between us.' She moved

down the aisle. 'Better pay for these before they think I'm lifting the stuff.'

'They've got their own security man here,' said Rewley, focusing into the middle distance at a row of tinned fish. 'That's him over there, trying to look interested in sardines... There's one of Drimwade's team here too, that woman in the dark tweed suit: I recognize her, Lesley Fitton. There must be something going on here.'

'There usually is, isn't there?' said Charmian indifferently. 'And probably a load of kids at it.' If she had to admit it, she rather liked the idea that Drimwade had problems and was overworked. But all the same she stood there, watching. Two youngsters pelted through the shoppers, pursued by Lesley Fitton, but they were out of the door and down the street before anyone could catch them. 'Well, that pair got away.'

She led the way to the coffee shop, where she sat down while Rewley went to get their cups and cream. He took his black, she noticed. He looked thinner today.

'How are you sleeping?' she asked.

'Alone.'

'I know that. A pity.'

She really meant it, he thought. Charmian was a surprise: sometimes almost puritanical, at other times amazingly open-minded. 'It's not too bad and as for what you mean...' He shrugged. 'I sleep enough.'

A liar, she thought, but a polite one. 'You could cut down on the coffee.'

'It's better than whisky.'

She looked at him with understanding. 'I'm not

saying it'll get better because it won't, but it'll change.' Grief did, after a while, it changed shape and fitted itself round you in a way you could live with.

Rewley drank some coffee. 'Wouldn't be so bad if Anny would let me have the child, but she won't – yet.'

'It'll work out. Your promotion will help. You can get a bigger place.'

'I couldn't afford two nurses and a nursery suite.'

Charmian was silent. The child was wealthy; her money in trust could pay for whatever was needed, but pride and misery were acting the devil inside Rewley.

I don't want to lose you, Rewley, she thought.

He had dressed in a hurry that morning; his shirt and tie were at war with each other, and he had shaved clumsily, leaving a trace of dried blood on his chin.

'I have the tape,' she said, 'but I want you to go through the whole interview for me now . . . What you saw, what you heard, and what you made of him.'

She listened quietly, occasionally putting in a word.

At the end she said, 'Thank you.' Then she was quiet. 'I wanted to hear it in your own words.' She finished her coffee. 'My turn now.' She told Rewley how Fanny had spent the night. 'I'm going there myself tonight. Something's going on.'

Rewley frowned. 'I'm not sure I like the sound of all this. Want me to come too?'

Charmian looked down at her hands. 'Yes, I'd like you to come . . .'

Rewley thought: She's a married woman, she loves her husband, and I loved my Kate. In addition, she's my boss . . .

Oh, God, life was not easy.

'But no,' said Charmian, raising her head. 'No.' She stood up. 'Better go.'

In silence they moved towards the exit, where their way was obstructed by a woman clutching a small child by the hand and pushing a trolley loaded with groceries. Another child sat on the trolley busily excavating her shopping.

The boy grabbed an orange and threw it at Rewley; he caught it and threw it back. The boy grinned but his mother ploughed on, looking at no one. She got through the door before them when Rewley stood aside politely to let Charmian go first.

Charmian stopped. 'Wait a minute, hang on... Look out there.'

Across the road Fanny and Frank Felyx were standing together, deep in conversation.

'Now what does that mean?' said Charmian. 'What are they up to?'

She saw Frank talking earnestly to Fanny, who was not saying much, except every so often she wagged a finger at him.

A large truck passed down the road, blocking their view, and when it had gone Charmian and Rewley saw Fanny preparing to go one way and Frank the other.

Chapter Six

Later on that very Wednesday and on to Thursday

Charmian and Rewley, close behind her, reached the pavement just as Frank and Fanny were splitting up. They halted to look at Charmian. Not exactly pleased or welcoming.

'Hello, Frank, you and Fanny having a little chat?'

He was gruff. 'Not exactly my choice. Listen I've made a statement about the shoe to Drimwade and his boys, I've been questioned once again by you and Dolly Barstow, my house has been inspected and searched, but I haven't been charged with anything and I was told I was free to take a walk so long as I didn't leave Windsor.'

'And you are taking a walk?'

'I had to buy some food, just like you.' He stared at Charmian's carrier bag. 'I had the bad luck to run into this lady here.' He looked down at Fanny who had prudently kept quiet. 'Not sure what she was buying, but something liquid, I daresay.'

'Just having a word with Frank,' Fanny said, seeing that something was expected of her. 'I wanted some milk for tonight.'

'I'll talk to you later,' Charmian answered, not with-

THE WOMAN WHO WAS NOT THERE

out menace. She looked down the road to where Ethel and Paulina could be seen emerging from the shop, each carrying a shopping bag.

'There they are,' said Frank. 'The other old witches.'

'Where's Dorie?' asked Charmian, as Ethel and Paulina saw them and hesitated.

'Working. She's doing a commercial, voice-over for a new milky drink.' Dorie excelled at doing children's voices, even a baby crying could be rendered plausibly and even charmingly by her.

'And that's not milk they're carrying,' growled Frank.

'Something for tonight.' A defensive murmur from Fanny.

Charmian knew what she was being told: Fanny was bringing her supporting bottle of brandy. Or would it be whisky tonight? 'I'll see you later,' she said.

Charmian sat slumped against the wall at the bottom of the stairs in Waxy House, her rug wrapped round her. She was thinking. Fanny was stretched out at the top of the stairs, silent but breathing heavily.

'You needn't come,' she had said to Fanny. 'If anything happens I'll tell you.'

'Of course you will. But I'd rather be there.'

It was dark in the house and cold; the chill was more intense in some areas than in others. 'Oh, haunted houses are like that,' Fanny had said happily. 'It's well known, we can take it as confirmation.'

I wonder, Charmian had thought; she preferred natural, realistic explanations for unusual phenomena.

'And the smell?' That seemed stronger in some areas of the house than in others. Like the hall, and the stairway. She had gone over the house with a torch when she came to find Fanny already there; Fanny's smell was a mixture of Miss Dior and whisky, with tincture of peppermint.

'I can't smell it now,' said Fanny, preparing to walk upstairs to make her nest for the night. 'I daresay I've got used to it.'

She took another peppermint.

Charmian felt like saying: Fanny dear, if you think the peppermint masks the smell of alcohol, then you're wrong. In my opinion, it draws attention to it.

The house had its smell, though. A strange smell, earthy yet astringent, not one smell exactly but a compound. The smells jostled for supremacy, with first one and then the other coming out on top, as the nose sorted them out. It was possible that underneath was yet another smell, darker, grimmer.

She crept up the stairs to see how Fanny was surviving on the top landing. She found her comfortably seated on cushions, with a shawl round her shoulders and a rug over her legs. She was raising a glass to her lips. The whole scene was lit up by a candle in a glass funnel.

Fanny jumped. 'You shouldn't steal up on a person like that,' she said crossly. 'Might have given me a heart attack.'

'I came to see how you were.'

'Now you see.'

Charmian looked at Fanny. 'Do you really believe

that something supernatural happens in this house? Or did you just say so in order to get me here?'

Fanny considered. 'Let's say half and half.'

'So nothing happened?'

'Oh, something happened all right. You'll see.'

'If there's a repeat performance.'

'Oh, go away and think about life.' She held out the bottle of whisky. 'Want a swig?'

'No.' Charmian went back down the stairs, passing the large looking-glass on the middle landing wall on the way to her own rug and pillow in the hall. She sat down, closed her eyes and prepared to follow Fanny's advice.

She closed her eyes because she wanted to think over what Rewley had had to say about his interview with coach driver, Arthur Doby.

Doby had been lurking behind the front door – at least Rewley said it had looked like lurking – of his South London flat. He had called it a maisonette, but it was a tiny, one-bedroom apartment of no beauty and some dirt, the top floor of a small suburban house. The hall and stairs leading to Doby's place were clean enough, so the downstairs tenant must be a better hand at housekeeping.

Well, more than dirt, she could hear Rewley saying, disorder and litter and the smell of dead mice. Possibly a live mouse or two. No, correct that, a whole bloody nest of them.

The WPC who had accompanied Rewley into the Lower Greenwich Road establishment had flinched at the rustlings and scufflings, but had stood her ground.

The place smelt of too much frying oil, often burnt

and stale to begin with, too much cigarette smoke, and too much living, all of the wrong sort.

But the man himself, Art Doby – 'Call me Art' – was clean enough in blue jeans, a checked shirt and a tweed jacket. Unpressed but washed. Shaved as well, although judging by a photograph on a table he had once had a beard, long and straggly. Rewley said he looked better without it. And the man, seeing his eyes on the picture, explained that his beard was seasonal. That in the winter when the coach company laid him off and he took temporary work as a long-distance lorry driver, then he had a beard. In spring and summer the coach company said their clients preferred him shaven. Beard discrimination, in short, but Doby gave way because the pay was good and he liked the places he drove to: Windsor, Oxford, Bath.

'All on rivers,' Rewley had said, to see how it took him. He did not react. A cool customer, or stupid, or innocent, unknowing of the shoe by Runnymede.

But which? The WPC thought him just stupid, but Rewley, observing a twitch of the lips, had thought him knowing and evil.

'He was a deity, that one,' Rewley said to Charmian. 'And worships at the shrine, a creditor in wickedness.'

It was not like Rewley to be poetical, and Charmian found his words echoing in her mind. She felt she was brushed on all sides of wickedness just now. Perhaps she attracted it instead of repelling it, pushing away, as she had always thought she had done, in her small way.

But it's a web, really, she thought dreamily, pouring herself a mug of coffee from her Thermos flask. The strands of good and evil are spun together, hard to separate.

Rewley's words sounded in her ear; she saw what he had seen. Doby had smiled at his two visitors, offered them seats on the sagging sofa, not minded when the WPC had cautiously moved a pile of papers to see what was underneath before she sat down. Underneath had been a plastic display card with some coins placed on it. He had grinned at her little frown when a hard-porn mag fell on to the floor. But he had said nothing.

On questioning by Rewley, he had said that, yes, it was a regular trip to Windsor, once a week, out in the morning, back in the early evening. His coach load was usually made up of tourists, Londoners out for the day, or people like Alicia, visiting a friend.

Another grin at this point, one inviting Rewley to ask whom was she visiting and for what purpose. Now Charmian could hear Rewley's voice telling her: Doby knew what she was, or had been, and he was letting me know. When he was shown a picture of Alicia Ellendale he recognized her at once. Said he had seen her before. And yes, he thought she had been a passenger on his coach.

And then he said: she's been down to Windsor on my coach a couple of times before. Visiting a pal, she said. And she named the man. Felix, she said. But don't think of a cat. Well, I'd come across Frank Felyx, so I reckoned I knew who she meant. Right, I said. Look out for me, she said, I'm a lady on a mission. Right, I said to her, making a joke of it, will do. My passengers do sometimes leave me odd little jobs to do, post a letter, look after a bit of luggage if they don't want to carry it around. It's part of my job to be a friendly chap.

Rewley had said to Charmian: I made him repeat those words about visiting someone called Felix. Rewley had gone on to say that he hadn't liked Doby but he had believed him. The WPC, an experienced officer, had agreed. The words had the ring of truth.

And what had happened when she hadn't returned? Rewley had asked.

Art Doby, showing yellow teeth in a smile, had said that he had waited, but had not been able to wait too long because the other passengers got restless and wanted to be on their way. 'Left to myself,' he had said, 'I would have gone on waiting a bit longer but they were a testy lot, my coach load that day, and I had to move. Anyway, the coach station itself was crowded and I needed to get out.'

And did you report her missing?

'No, because she was a grown-up lady who knew her own business. Again that grin,' Rewley said. 'I was getting to kind of hate that grin.'

Rewley had questioned Doby on when he had learned that a search was being made for Alicia.

Didn't know, Doby had answered, 'but the word began to get around, I was making jokes, they were only jokes then, about Frank Felyx, but then a copper came to the coach station asking questions... Her shoe had been found with a foot, her foot, in it. I remembered what she'd said about visiting Felix. Frank Felyx, I thought, and I thought, I bet he did it.'

'We were sitting in that stinking room,' Rewley had

said, 'and I found myself disliking the man intensely. And afterwards the WPC said he gave her the creeps. But we both agreed that he was telling us what had happened. He was a liar, I'd say a born liar, but even liars tell the truth.' He had looked down at his hands. 'I felt like washing myself when we left. Not just imagination, that, either; the smell of the place hung on my clothes . . . You'll probably smell it on the report I wrote afterwards.'

Charmian thought she got a snatch of it now, but the smell of Waxy House was overpowering. But you didn't know about the shoe in the bin in the washroom, then, she said silently to Rewley. I'd like to know what Art Doby could make of that.

And he was a man with a collection of coins. Had he been the source of the sovereign left on the table? That would tie him to whatever was going on in Waxy House. She found she was keen that he should be tied in, and the two affairs linked. It would make for symmetry.

She drank her coffee.

'All right up there, Fanny?' she called.

'Doing fine,' Fanny called back.

'All quiet so far.'

'You wait. It'll get going.' The whisky-cheerful voice carried on: 'I'm not a fool, you know. I heard what I heard.'

'Didn't see, though.'

'No, praise be. I had my holy water, didn't I? Sprinkled it around me in a ring, so I could hear but couldn't see.'

'And anyway you had your eyes closed,' called

Charmian up the staircase. Silence, which showed her she had scored.

When nothing happened within the next hour, she became irritated with herself for coming to Waxy House at all. Nothing was going to happen, nothing had happened, nothing could happen. Fanny had imagined it all.

Not like Fanny, though; there was a hard core of realism inside her.

Up the stairs came the soft faint sound of a ladylike snore.

Her own eyes closed.

Just as she was dropping off to sleep, she realized that the smell of the house had changed. A new smell was creeping into her nostrils, waking her as surely as a cold touch on the face.

She sat up straight, moving quietly. The house was dark; Fanny must have put out the candle. After a moment she realized that the quality of the darkness itself had changed. The darkness had never been absolute because light from the street lamps filtered through the windows.

She sat there taking in the breath of chill air. She turned her head to the front door, but it remained closed. The coldness was on her other cheek and the smell was growing stronger.

It was the smell of the tomb, she told herself with a shudder: damp, earthy and stony.

She stood up, turning towards the stairs. The change in the light, the smell, seemed to be coming from there. Slowly, carefully, she mounted the stairs, and as she did so she saw the darkness was greyer and the smell stronger with every step. Was there yet another element in that smell?

The light, if it was light, seemed to move. Distantly, she heard the sound of movements. A dry rustle.

She stopped; she felt as if she had received a blow to her chest. Then, steadying herself, she started to walk up the stairs, stepping very carefully.

There was a rustle again on the stair above her, out of sight round the curve of the staircase. The air moved, she could feel it on her cheek.

Then Fanny screamed. A piercing scream. 'Someone's here!'

'I'm coming, Fanny.' Charmian rushed up the staircase, struggling to see in the gloom.

Fanny wailed: 'Something touched me!'

When Charmian got there, Fanny was lighting a candle. 'Blood!' she cried. 'Someone, something left blood behind.'

Bright red, new blood. Not dried old blood.

Charmian said, 'It's your own.' There was a long cut down Fanny's cheek. She looked around her. On the floor was a broken glass. 'You cut yourself, you must have broken the glass when you threshed around screaming . . . and then cut yourself.'

'I didn't break the glass.'

'Well, you had a nightmare, did it then, Fanny dear.'

'Someone touched me,' said Fanny doggedly.

Charmian helped the other woman to her feet. 'Come on, we'll sit together downstairs.'

Fanny collected her possessions carefully and let herself be led away. They made themselves comfortable on the assembled rugs and cushions and Charmian poured out what was left of her coffee. 'Still warm,' she said.

Neither of them mentioned what had happened. Although both thought a presence had been in Waxy House, they would not have agreed on the nature of it.

Not a ghost, nothing spooky, but man-made, somehow, Charmian thought.

'Don't worry,' she said as she drove Fanny home in the early morning, both of them feeling exhausted. 'Forget Waxy House and whatever is going on there. It won't hurt you. Just stay away till things clear up.'

'What things?'

'I don't know, but I'll find out. If I have to tear the place to pieces.'

Fanny looked shocked at this threat to her inheritance. 'You'd have to ask my permission first.'

'No, I wouldn't . . . It would depend.'

'On what?'

'On what I might be looking for,' said Charmian, stopping the car. 'Here you are, Fanny. Home. Have a hot bath and a good breakfast. It's what I'm going to do.'

'And then the day off?'

'No, you know better than that. I have plenty to do. You aren't my only problem.'

Although Fanny and Charmian had left early in the morning, their presence had not gone unnoticed. The two one-man firms, C. and C. Architects and Computer Wizard, both started work very early for personal reasons. It suited both Christopher Fenwick (especially while his wife was away), and Harry Aden, aka Daddy Christmas.

'There's a zombie in there,' said Chris Fenwick, nodding towards Waxy House.

'Oh, come on.' Harry was locking his car. 'What's a zombie?'

'I don't know for sure. The undead, they say. Sound and movement, I say, and not form.'

Harry looked at his neighbour, wondering if he was joking. You could never be sure with Chris Fenwick.

'Or it might be Frank Felyx,' said Chris with a grin.

'You don't like him?'

'Not a lot. He's always taken an interest in the house. Wanted to buy it.' Chris laughed. 'Asked my advice . . . Don't know what he planned to do with it. A little hotel for undead, perhaps.'

'But he didn't buy it?'

'No, I don't know why. May not have been on the market. Or perhaps he hadn't got the money.'

Charmian had a bath, fed the cat and drank some coffee. Any more nights like last night and she would have caffeine poisoning. She had seen Fanny to her door before going home herself. Fanny looked quite chirpy. She felt she had been vindicated: Charmian now knew that 'things' did happen in Waxy House. No more jokes and sceptical looks, please.

Charmian's next problem was how to see the boy Angus Cairns, with or without his father. She had learned that there was no mother, not in residence, at least.

Well, Dr Cairns had a practice, in Merrywick as she believed, so he could be contacted. She left a message for her secretary to arrange an early appointment for her to see him and the boy before she went to London. She wanted to talk to Angus about what he had found before she saw Art Doby.

By the time she was out of the bath and dressed, an appointment had been arranged. 'As soon as you can this morning, as the boy ought to get to school. And Dr Cairns wants to meet you.'

Charmian was surprised; she knew that she was not always welcome when she was engaged in an investigation. She had a formidable reputation. It was to be hoped she did not disappoint Dr Cairns.

She went to her office first, to check on messages, faxes, and post – she had learnt early in her career to keep abreast of information, queries and complaints – then she drove herself to Merrywick.

The Cairns lived in a bungalow in a quiet suburban road, lined with well polished motorcars. The car parked in the drive of Cairn House was a green Mercedes.

Doing all right, Charmian deduced.

A boy's bike, by no means as well polished, was propped against a rose bush. A man stood in the large front window, then he was joined by a boy.

'Ah, my victim,' she said, wondering why she had chosen that word.

When the front door was opened, by the boy, she was ready with her hand outstretched and friendly smile. 'Ah, Angus . . . It is Angus?'

THE WOMAN WHO WAS NOT THERE

'Yes.' He did not smile back; instead he looked serious.

Dr Cairns appeared behind his son. 'Come in, come in.' He was a tall, stalwart, broad-shouldered man with a military air. Perhaps he had been a soldier once, but at all events he was now in general practice and was a police surgeon.

'I thought you would want to see Angus. Once I knew you were handling the case.'

'You knew?'

'Oh, we all know, ma'am.' Yes, he had been a soldier once, no doubt of it. 'And delighted to hear it.' He turned to the boy. 'Bring the tray in, lad. I've made some coffee and was just about to drink it. Will you join me?'

The tray was neatly arranged with a coffee pot, a jug of milk and two cups. There was a mug for the boy. He drank milk. 'He can have coffee one day but not yet,' said his father.

'You make good coffee . . .' It was hot and strong.

'Had to learn. I'm on my own these days and anyway my former wife never could make decent coffee.'

The boy sat on a low chair, sipping his mug of milk without much appearance of pleasure. Charmian hoped he would be admitted to the senior ranks of coffee drinkers soon.

'I've been longing to meet you since I attended a lecture you gave here a couple of years ago: "Murder in the Community", you called it,' continued Cairns senior.

'I remember.' In fact, the title had been chosen by

the organizer of the lecture series, of which her talk had been only one and which she had thought was a bit glib. 'I'm glad you enjoyed it.'

'You're such a good speaker, and you made some good points.'

'Thank you.' She wanted to bring this part of the conversation to an end. Dr Cairns was overdoing it.

'Dad,' said the boy.

His father took no notice. 'Of course, I was not a police surgeon then, although I had leanings that way. Didn't take it up until I lost my wife . . . Didn't seem the sort of thing to do with a wife and family. You're called out at odd times. Well, you know all about that.'

Charmian nodded.

Dr Cairns finally brought the conversation round to the matter in hand. 'It's the first time that I've discovered a murder exhibit myself,' he said.

'It was me that found it,' Angus piped up.

His father ignored him. 'Of course, we haven't got the rest of the body yet . . . I'm assuming there is one. You can lose a foot and survive.'

'Perhaps not in this case.'

'No, I agree. It was a butcher's job, you know. Worse, really; a competent butcher would have been neater. This foot was hacked off.'

Charmian bent towards the boy whom she thought was being ignored by his father. 'Your discovery was very important. I expect your father has explained it to you. Don't let it alarm you. Tell me how you happened to see the shoe.'

Angus stood up. 'I was writing a poem; we did

THE WOMAN WHO WAS NOT THERE

Tennyson at school, and I enjoy doing it, and it was about the river. So I was watching as on one of my walks... And I just saw the shoe.' He paused. 'I could see it was a bit more than a shoe, I mean it didn't look empty.' He paused again. 'Well, I could see the ankle and a bit of stocking... a bit bloody.'

'I believe the foot came from a corpse,' said Dr Cairns. 'So there wouldn't be much blood.'

'I didn't mind it, you know, I was just interested. Only...' Angus paused once again.

'Yes?' said Charmian.

'Only afterwards, when you think about things...'

'I know. When you think about a find like that, in bed, at night, perhaps, you do get darker thoughts,' said Charmian with sympathy, ignoring several huffs and puffs from the good doctor, a parent who clearly expected his child to conform to certain rules. Not a sensitive man, and the son might be. 'I'd like to see your poem.'

'I haven't finished it yet, I'm writing a new one.'

'Perhaps I could see that one, then?'

Angus produced a notebook, which he handed over. 'I've only just begun it, I can't move forward.'

'Poems are like that. I don't know much about writing poetry, but I do know that much. I expect it'll come.'

'Yeah.' He cast his eyes down and looked thoughtful. 'Don't ask what it's about, though, will you?'

'No, I know better than to do that.' She opened the book and read to herself:

'Boys and girls come to play.

*If we may, but who will pay.
So run away.'*

'I haven't got any further. Perhaps I never will. You can't tell with poems, sometimes they die.' He looked at Charmian with big, solemn brown eyes. She thought this poem meant something important to him.

'If you ever finish it, perhaps you'll let me read it,' she said, handing the book back.

At the bottom of the page the word BLACK was scrawled, then crossed through. She didn't make much of that, so she passed it over.

Angus was nodding slowly, almost to himself; he avoided looking at his father, who was frowning.

'Do you go to walk by the river often?'

'As often as I can.'

'I suppose people do drop this and that into the river.'

'From boats, mostly,' he said.

His father put in, half grudgingly, half proudly, 'The boy knows his river.'

'You've seen people throwing rubbish into the river?'

He shrugged. 'Sometimes. I mean I don't watch. It wouldn't interest me . . .' Then he added: 'I don't think the shoe can have been there for very long.'

'I agree.'

She met Dr Cairns' eyes; he gave a little nod. His judgement also.

'Because the rats would have started to chew it.'

'Yes,' Charmian accepted this judgement. As his father had said: the lad knew his river. 'I think so too. You've seen the rats, I suppose?'

THE WOMAN WHO WAS NOT THERE

Angus nodded slowly. 'I don't mind rats. The river is their home.'

Dr Cairns took up his theme once again of how much he admired Charmian's work, how he had read about her cases. How he had actually seen her before, years ago, when she first started police work in Deerham Hills. He had been a medical student himself, doing a term's ward work in the hospital there. They had had a murder. Well, more than one.

So they had, and Charmian decided not to think how long ago that had been. She let him talk himself out, while she finished her coffee, and then said goodbye.

She smiled at Angus, who gave her a very cautious smile back, suggesting that he was not as keen on Charmian Daniels as his father was, and thought perhaps she should be handled with care.

Charmian was satisfied as she got in the car and started it up: the boy had not seen the person who had left the shoe with the foot in it, he had come upon it by chance. It was what she had always thought. Tough father, though.

Yet there was something about the child that worried her. She felt he had something on his mind that he did not wish to share. Perhaps the presence of the father held him back? She wasn't sure if *she* would have wanted to unburden herself to Dr Cairns.

And where was the wife and mother? What did he mean by saying she was lost? Lost to death or just to him? None of her business, of course, but she could find out. It was the sort of information you could rely on Dolly Barstow to know, and she wanted to build up her picture of the family.

As she turned the car to drive away, Angus came to the gate and waved to her. 'Drowning or waving?' she asked herself as she waved back. A mixture of both, probably; it usually was. What a lot of applicants for help I have hanging on me, she thought, remembering Fanny and to a lesser extent Rewley. And I think I just picked up another one there.

Dolly Barstow said: 'Oh yes, the story is his wife just packed her bags and left him. That's one version. Another is that he packed her bags and threw her out. And yet another story says he packed her in a trunk and left her to be collected at a railway station. Brighton, I think. She hasn't been found yet.' Dolly was driving them swiftly down the motorway to London, having insisted that it was her job to do the driving. 'A fond father, though.'

'Not a popular man, I gather.'

'Not so very.'

'Why?'

Dolly drove some distance in silence. 'Don't know. Perhaps some men are born to be disliked.' Then she turned to Charmian with a grin. 'Oh, all right, people think he's too much an I-and-I-and-I man, you know what I mean, and doesn't give others due credit. But he's a good doctor, no one disputes that.'

Clever, arrogant and therefore resented by his peers. Low on charm, was Charmian's assessment. The boy still troubled her, though.

THE WOMAN WHO WAS NOT THERE

'So what about Fanny Fanfairly?' enquired Dolly as she steered them through the traffic. 'What happened? Tell me.'

Charmian gave her a careful summary of what had gone on in Waxy House, being neither dramatic nor passing over the strangeness of it all.

'There was a presence, sure of it. If I had been a bit quicker, or possibly a bit slower, I would have caught the person.'

'But where did he or she go?'

'I wish I knew. Out of the window, for all I could tell.'

'And why? What's it all about?'

'I wish I knew that too. But it's aimed at Fanny somehow.'

Then they were both silent with the traffic heavy as Dolly drove along the motorway in her usual concentrated fashion. Charmian was thinking about Fanny and Frank and the woman Alicia, still missing but presumed to be dead.

They drove off the motorway; she let her eyes dwell with pleasure on the terrace of Victorian artists' studios with their splendid, tall and decorative windows on the way to Kensington. Did artists still live and paint in them? She had heard that a few did.

Then they were speeding past the big spread of the Victoria and Albert Museum, past the Brompton Oratory on their left and then Harrods on the right. Into Piccadilly and turning down the river and Westminster Bridge and out towards the grubby suburbs of South London. Once unfashionable as somewhere to live, this was changing, as Dolly pointed out.

They were not yet smart, but with the middle classes desperate to find living space near the city centre that was cheap (or cheaper – nowhere was really cheap any more, unless it had no roof and dry rot in the basement), and which could be converted into something 'charming' with not too much trouble, this fate would soon be upon them. And from 'quaint' and 'friendly' and 'full of charm when you looked at them with imagination', they would soon become downright expensive.

Charmian had worked in the capital for a short space but she did not know South London well. However, Dolly had been at university in London and had lived not far from where the coach driver had his home. 'Nine of us rented a large house in Peckham,' Dolly said. 'It had a lot of advantages apart from size because it was on a good bus route and close to a lovely street market where the vegetables and fish were fresh and cheap. You could even buy meat and poultry, but we couldn't afford that often. One stall sold delicious sausages... I can remember them now. I expect it's all changed. When we moved out the house was bought by a pop star. That shows you!'

Charmian looked at the address on a card. 'Three Draper Street, off Newbank Road. Mean anything to you?'

'No, but I have a map. I'll choose a quiet spot and stop to read it. I think I remember where Newbank Road was. The trouble is, if I remember aright, it's enormously long with a railway station in it. Still, that should make it easier to find. You can't hide a railway station.'

She studied the road ahead. 'And in fact, I think I may be getting close. There's a sign and an arrow pointed right: railway station.' She swung the car. 'So we'll go this way and, yes, this is Newbank Road. Hasn't changed much.'

Newbank Road looked as though it hadn't in fact changed since the Victorian builders of the railway had moved out so that the new housing terraces could go up. Gentrification had not yet set in around here.

Dolly drew into the kerb to study her map; a large van that had been following her hooted angrily and swerved out into the centre road. Dolly ignored this sally, except to say: 'Rude lot round here.'

Charmian wound down the window to let in a wind heavy with dust, bits of paper, and smelling of frying oil and curry. Somewhere close there had to be an Indian restaurant. 'You know this district, I don't.'

'Like a lot of London: large areas of decent streets with pockets here and there where every vice and every crime can find a home to breathe. You just have to get to learn which is which. The locals point the way.'

'And Draper Street?'

'Don't know yet. Newbank Road is acceptable if you don't mind living on the top of all the traffic, but after a while you don't notice the noise and the smell.'

'Not even the stale curry?'

Dolly shook her head. 'No, you probably smell like it yourself, you see, and everyone knows you can't smell your own smell . . . Just as well, sometimes.' She started the car and drove on, getting a hoot from another car as she drew out. 'Palmer Street first, then Draper Street.'

Charmian watched the houses pass: respectable worlds, criminal worlds, easy worlds, difficult worlds. Dolly could live in each and survive. She herself no longer could. It was marriage that did it. It changed your constitution, weakened you. Being part of another person was not a strength as was often supposed: it was a division.

Dolly swung round into Draper Street, a street of modest brick houses, the kerb lined with parked cars. 'Even numbers this side.' Dolly turned her head towards the other side of the road. 'Odd over there, but the numbers are high.' She had excellent long-distance sight. 'So number three must be at the end of the road. It's a dead end, you can't drive through.'

'What do you make of Draper Street?' Charmian looked about her. Plenty of rubbish blowing up and down the street, but the curtains on most windows seemed clean, and the front doors tidy.

Dolly drove slowly up the road, assessing it. 'Midway to respectable. It's going up in the world, I think. The houses get grubbier and more unpainted as we come this way, but one or two are for sale. Been down, going up, I'd say.'

'Would you live here?'

Dolly didn't answer. She had parked the car in an empty slot and was looking up at number three. 'Let into flats,' she pronounced. 'Furnished, I should guess. Minimally furnished so the landlord can regain possession if need be. And would I live here?' She shrugged. 'If I had to, wouldn't kill me.' Charmian, she thought to herself, had got soft. Marriage contributing. You couldn't expect her ladyship to live in a near slum, even one that was rising in the world.

'I want to think for a minute.' Then Charmian said: 'I need to talk about this affair. I think the man we are going to see may have killed Alicia Ellendale. I think he's a killer. I don't know the motive, or where and how she died. Or where she is now. But I believe she is dead and I believe he may have killed her ... Evidence is hard to come by, so you could say I'm going on feeling.'

'What did Rewley think?'

'Good question. He didn't like Arthur Doby.'

'Doesn't prove he's a killer.'

'Of course not.' Charmian was silent. 'There's something else. An odd fact that must fit in somehow. A sovereign was left in Waxy House. Not there one night, somehow there the next morning.'

'So?'

'Rewley says Doby collects coins.'

'You are tying him in with Waxy House?' asked Dolly incredulously; she was so surprised that she hit the car horn with her hand and it gave a melancholy little toot.

'I don't know what I'm doing,' admitted Charmian. 'Hope to get things clearer after I see Doby himself.'

Dolly looked up at the house. 'Two flats there, as far as I can see. How do we get in? Are we expected?'

'Rewley arranged that the local WPC detective who came with him would be here today and that she would set up the meeting. I believe Doby is there. I spoke to her on the phone before we left.' Charmian studied the road. 'I expected to see her here.'

'There she is now,' said Dolly, nodding towards a tall young woman in uniform who had got out of a car parked ahead of them and was walking towards them. Charmian first and then Dolly Barstow got out of the car.

'WPC Mary Carter . . .' the girl said; she really was not much more, with dark curls and big brown eyes. 'I was told to expect you, ma'am. I sort of keep an eye on this area, it's my responsibility, that's why I was told off for this particular meeting.'

'You met Inspector Rewley yesterday.'

'Yes, sure.' She gave a wide smile. Rewley had clearly made an impact.

'Doby expecting us?'

'Sure is. I made it clear you would be here today with me. He said he would be home.'

'Good. Well done.' Charmian introduced Dolly Barstow. 'Inspector Barstow. Working with me on this case.'

Dolly acknowledged the introduction; she thought the girl looked bright and keen. She looked up at the window of number three. 'Top floor flat, I believe? Is he a man of his word, will he be there?'

'I don't know if I would call him that, but I laid it down clear and firm. Yes, I think we'll find him home.'

'What sort of a man is he?'

Mary Carter looked cautious. 'I don't know him well, just observed him from a distance.'

'Liked by the neighbours and the people he worked with?'

'I don't think he's loved, exactly.' Then she gave a

wide grin. 'In fact, I heard one neighbour call him a mean, cruel old sod.'

Charmian looked up and down the street. 'I suppose we're being watched?'

'I expect so,' said Mary Carter cheerfully. 'It's usual. I never know whether the neighbours just like each other so much they have to know what goes on, or whether they can't bear to miss anything.'

'Well, let's get in, shall we, ma'am?' said Dolly.

Charmian nodded, leading the way to the house. Two door bells, one above the other, with the upper one labelled DOBY. She pressed this bell.

No answer. Silence. No movement inside.

Charmian rang again.

'Should be there,' said Mary Carter, her cheerfulness still in place.

The three women waited in silence. 'I can hear someone coming,' said Mary Carter.

The front door opened to let out a young woman pushing a small pram in which lay a silent, red-faced baby. The mother was red-faced too, with a fringe of dark hair and a plump little body in jeans and sweater. She seemed surprised to see a reception committee.

'Oh, hello, you looking for me?' She took in Mary Carter's uniform with some alarm. 'Anything wrong? Not my husband? He's not had an accident?'

'No, no, Mrs Darby,' said Charmian, reading the name from the card above the lower bell. 'We want the man in the top flat: Mr Doby.'

Mrs Darby rolled her eyes. 'Might have guessed. Well, good luck to you. I'll leave you to it.' She began to push and the baby, sensing his moment, set up a wail. 'Shut up, you.'

'Is Mr Doby there?'

'Couldn't say. I keep out of his way. But I heard someone on the stairs – going out. I think.'

'Thank you, we'll go in. Is there a bell on the upstairs door?'

'A knocker.' Mrs Darby was out of the house and on to the pavement. 'Bang it hard, I would.'

One behind the other, they went up the narrow stair to Doby's personal and private front door. There was a black knocker with which Charmian gave a loud double knock.

No one came. 'He's usually slow,' said Mary Carter. 'Never keen to open the door. I don't think he likes people.'

Dolly Barstow had leaned back against the narrow banister while she waited.

'Knock again,' she advised.

Charmian did so. 'He may have gone out, damn him.'

Dolly was staring down at her hand. 'I rubbed this on the banister...' A red streak lay across her palm. 'This is blood.'

Charmian stared down at Dolly's hand, then turned to Mary Carter. 'We've got to get in there. Get help for us to break in.'

Silently Mary Carter nodded. She went down the stairs and out to the car. Presently, she came back. 'I phoned through. A support car is on the way.'

But Charmian had been thinking. 'Wait a minute... People often leave a key under the mat in case they get shut out . . . She lifted the rubber mat in front of the door. Nothing.

But there was blood seeping through the door and round the mat.

'We must get in quickly.' She ran her hand round the lintel at the top of the door. 'Something here . . .' She drew her hand away, holding out a key. 'I'm going in.'

The key turned easily in the lock. Charmian pushed. 'Something's blocking the door.' Dolly came up and gave the door a shove, which gave way grudgingly, offering enough room for Charmian to slide through.

Once inside, she looked down at the body that had been partly blocking the door.

A man lay there, on his back at an angle to the door, with blood staining his throat and chest. She knelt down beside him. The body was still warm, but he was not breathing. With that wound in his throat, death would have come soon.

'It's Doby, I think. He's had his throat cut.'

Chapter Seven

Still on Thursday

The man, Arthur Doby, lay on his back. His eyes were open and staring at the ceiling. The ceiling must have been the last thing he saw. Blood had stained his shirt, streamed down on to his jeans and spilled over on the floor.

Mary Carter, who had put in her call to the local CID, was standing at the door staring at what she saw. 'Sergeant Edwards will be here soon,' she was saying, 'on his way now. My goodness.'

Charmian straightened up. 'He's not cold.' Nor had he stiffened; rigor had not set in. Various factors influenced the onset of rigor, but she was sure Doby had not been dead long. 'I thought he was the killer, and now he's been murdered himself.'

'He knew who the killer was, then,' said Dolly Barstow.

Charmian was walking round the room. It was as squalid as Rewley had described. This had been Doby's living room, with a large sofa on which he seemed to have deposited a good deal of his wardrobe, dirty shirts, a pair of grey flannel trousers and some underpants. A check jacket was draped over an arm of the sofa. In

THE WOMAN WHO WAS NOT THERE

the middle of the room was a square table on which the remains of several meals could be seen.

'Frank Felyx accused him and he accused Frank.'

'You still have your other candidate, then.'

Charmian stared at the blood which was still liquid. 'The blood hasn't congealed.'

'No. Not dead many minutes, then.' Dolly too was staring at Doby's body. 'He looks a strong man. How do you cut the throat of a strong man without him fighting you off?'

'You come up behind him and stick the knife in.' She added, 'And then pull it across the throat.'

'But wouldn't you get blood on you?'

'You would indeed... Mrs Darby heard someone on the stairs; it must have been Doby's killer leaving.'

'Pity she didn't look out.'

'I don't know about that... This murderer is ruthless, he might have killed her too.'

'He must have been fully as tall as Doby, probably taller, in order to get the knife into that position.'

The two women looked at each other. Frank Felyx was strong and tall, taller than Doby. 'I don't want to believe the murderer is Frank Felyx,' Charmian said.

Into the silence that followed, Dolly said: 'No weapon. I don't see a knife anywhere.'

'I had a quick look, but it could be here. A search might turn it up. We can't touch anything. The local CID will be here soon with the SOCO, and photographers and the lot. All we can do is stand and watch... And they won't want us to do that for very long.' She was well aware that her appearance here would not be welcome.

From her place by the door, Mary Carter said: 'I hear them, ma'am. Sounds like Sergeant Edwards' voice.'

They could hear him running up the stairs, talking as he did so with a companion whom he was ordering to stay down at the door and to tell Mrs Darby what was happening but not to let her up.

Before the sergeant reached Doby's room, Charmian said to Dolly: 'Notice the coins?' She pointed to the table. 'By the loaf of bread on the dirty plate, a plastic envelope with coins. Part of his collection.'

Dolly nodded. 'Took it in.'

Charmian walked over. 'They interest me. I want to fit them in somewhere but I don't see how.'

'You think Doby was the source of the sovereign left in Waxy House?'

'It'd be neat. Hard to explain but neat. A bit of a jigsaw puzzle slotting into place. But I don't see how he left it in person.'

'Perhaps he sold it or gave it to whoever did?'

'At the moment the likeliest suspects are me and Fanny. We were the only ones with access to the house.'

'As far as you know.'

'As far as I know,' said Charmian with a frown. She was looking at another object on the table. She moved a newspaper aside so she could get a better look. 'What do you make of this photograph?'

Dolly came closer. 'A woman in a summer dress in front of a house . . . I suppose it could be Alicia Ellendale . . . It's like the photograph we were sent. Younger.'

'I think it *is* Alicia.'

THE WOMAN WHO WAS NOT THERE

'So Doby must have known her longer than he admitted.'

'I always thought there was more of a relationship than he admitted. But look at the house behind. It's not this house.'

'Where she lived? No,' said Dolly frowning.

'No. It's not very clear, but I think it's Waxy House.'

The sergeant came into the room quietly for a big man, and stood looking at them, then he turned for one more word with Mary Carter. 'The SOCO can come in but no one else just yet. Keep everyone else out,' he was saying.

Over her shoulder, as Charmian walked towards the door to greet the new arrivals, she said: 'I shan't say anything about coins to the sergeant, and don't you. Or the photograph.'

Dolly's eyebrows went up.

'Yes, I know. I'll let them know in the end. But I want to think things out.'

Sergeant Edwards was a fair-haired young man, with a long face, pale blue eyes and a broken nose. A rugger player, Charmian decided. Not a boxer, too tall and rangy. He had a slight Cockney accent, which was not unattractive. Against her expectations he was not hostile and, indeed, he seemed pleased to see her. 'Nice to meet you, ma'am; knew you were taking a hand in the Windsor end of our little trouble.'

He stalked into the room and took a good, long look at the dead Arthur Doby. He stared down and clicked his teeth. 'Oh dear, dear, not a pretty sight.' He shook his head. 'All the same, I wonder he wasn't done before.'

'You didn't like him.'

'Who did? No one. Although when he got himself up, he didn't look too bad. A one for the ladies.'

'Was he now?'

Edwards gave her an alert look. 'You're wondering about Alicia Ellendale? You're interested in her; so are we.'

'She may be alive, she may not be,' said Charmian, aware as she spoke that Dolly Barstow had moved towards the table where she was unobtrusively studying the envelope of coins. 'But she is certainly without a pair of shoes and one foot. I think she's dead.'

'She's dead,' said the sergeant with certainty. 'She was dead when that foot was cut off.'

'So they say.'

'I never met her myself, but she had quite a fan club round here...' His eyes narrowed with amusement. 'She was a purveyor of good information, you understand. My colleagues liked that.'

'Don't we all? Is that why you're so keen to find her and/or track down her killer?'

'Well, I understand,' he kept his voice cautiously down, as if imparting a secret, 'that when she went missing she was sitting on some very useful information that she was going to tell all about. The idea is she might have been kidnapped to stop her doing this.'

'Perhaps that's what happened.'

'Could be. Now it looks as though she's dead, so we're having to keep an open mind about it.'

'The man... I suppose it was a man... on whom she was going to drop the dirt, might have done it.'

'Well, difficult for him,' confessed Edwards. 'He's

banged up. He could have paid someone, but it doesn't seem likely.'

'What's he in for?'

'Rape, and she was going to tie him into a killing . . . Men like that don't have many friends inside.'

Charmian meditated on this truth. 'I had Doby down as Alicia's killer. His own murder makes this unlikely. Unless it has nothing to do with Alicia's disappearance, but I find this hard to believe. I don't care for coincidences.'

'Neater if you don't have them,' agreed Edwards obligingly.

'Inspector Barstow and I will get back to Windsor. I think the answer is there. We have to find the rest of Alicia, it's got to be somewhere.'

'You won't wait for a word with my boss? He'll be here any minute.'

'No need. We can talk on the phone. Tell him I've been and gone.'

'We'll need a statement,' suggested Edwards modestly.

'Send someone down.' She was pulling rank now.

Edwards paled a little but accepted what he could not refuse. There might be trouble about this, but on the whole not for him.

'The most virtuous thing about him was that he collected coins,' said Edwards. 'I don't know if you noticed.'

'I did notice.'

'Thought you had,' he grinned.

'And, of course, you will send me all the forensic

reports, and so on. Photographs, et cetera, as soon as you can.' Sooner, her voice said.

'Will do, ma'am.'

Charmian and Dolly Barstow escaped just as some more of the local CID team arrived. They saw her go and probably waved a couple of fingers at her.

'What do you make of Edwards?' asked Charmian as they drove away.

'Sharp.'

'Yes. I thought he was.'

'But we're sharp too.'

'True.' Charmian sat back in her seat. 'Wonder what he meant about the coin collection?'

'Probing.'

'Yes. Don't let's go back to Windsor yet. Let's stop and have lunch first. I want to think.' She looked out of the window. 'Know anywhere to eat round here?'

'No.' Dolly kept her eyes on the road.

'We'll go to the place I go to with my husband sometimes . . . It's on the way home.'

Knightsbridge, Dolly calculated accurately to herself as she drove. I'm devoted to Charmian, my boss, but how her standards have risen since she married. No dropping into little sandwich bars any more.

Charmian seemed to read her thoughts. 'It's quite modest, you'll see when we get there. I'll direct you once we're past Piccadilly.'

This she did with a right here, and a left there and finally: 'Here we are.'

Dolly looked out at a neat, brown-painted establishment with the name Fergus above in gold. You could see through the windows to tables of people eating.

THE WOMAN WHO WAS NOT THERE

You always know, she said to herself, that a restaurant with just one plain name like that is going to be expensive.

But she parked the car at the kerb and followed her boss in. Charmian sailed forward to be greeted by the proprietor, presumably Fergus himself, who certainly seemed to know and like her and called her by her married name.

'Right, Your Ladyship,' muttered Dolly.

But Charmian had been correct in her judgement: the food was simple but good. They both ordered an omelette and salad, and were allowed to drink no wine, but coffee with their meal.

Charmian pushed her coffee cup aside and put her elbows on the table. 'If that house is, as it looks to me, Waxy House, then it ties in Alicia and the house and what is going on there.'

'Perhaps she is its ghost,' said Dolly lightly. She was still troubled that Charmian had said nothing to Edwards. She thought: She's getting a bit above herself what with her marriage and being head of SRADIC. The old Charmian wouldn't have hung on to what might be important information, she would have told Edwards.

'If you believe in ghosts.'

'I don't.'

'Nor do I. Something real and horrible is happening in Waxy House, but I don't know more. I'm guessing.'

'Guessing what?'

Charmian took a deep breath. 'I guess that there is something in Waxy House that has to be protected. Fanny, the new owner, the only person to take an interest in the place for years, is to be kept out. Frightened out.'

'Fanny won't be frightened easily.'

'She is frightened, though, and who's to blame her? I was myself. She won't give up ownership, but she might give up possession, put the house up for sale.' She asked the waiter for some more coffee; suddenly she needed it. 'That's as far as I've got. Dead end.'

Dolly drank her own coffee and watched Charmian's face.

'And this is only for you, Dolly. It's not the sort of speculation I should pass around some of my other colleagues. I shall talk it over with Rewley, I can trust him.'

'Trust? Does that come into it?'

Charmian leaned forward. 'Think about it, Dolly. Police come into this: Felyx was one of us, Alicia was an informer . . . I know you think it was wrong of me not to tell Edwards all that is in my mind, but I want to be sure.'

'You don't trust Edwards?'

'I don't have any reason not to, but I want to see how events develop.'

'He seemed straight enough to me.' Dolly looked at Charmian and shook her head. 'Aren't you being super-sensitive about police involvement?'

'I certainly hope so.' Charmian waved a hand for the bill. When it arrived Dolly stretched out a hand too. 'I'm paying, Dolly.'

'I'll owe you,' said Dolly firmly. 'You can dine with me at home, one or both of you. I'm getting to be a good cook and I've got some decent wine.' She wasn't prepared to let Charmian play hostess.

'Accepted.' Charmian had the depressing feeling that her old easy relationship with Dolly was melting away somehow. Her fault or Dolly's?

Never had you down for one of the ruling class, lady-of-the-manor types, Dolly was saying to herself as she started the car; thought we were mates. She made a resolve: 'I'll see this case through, then I'll ask for a transfer to another posting, another area.' She looked at Charmian out of the corner of her eye and felt sad: life did bring you to partings. 'She's not noticing,' she said to herself sadly. 'She doesn't know at all how I feel.'

Friendship between women was a tricky business, Charmian mused as they sped down the motorway. In some ways harder to manage than the relationship between men and women: sex did loosen things up and if you hadn't got that to work off emotion and lighten a mood, where were you?

'I'd better tell you, Dolly, that I mean to go into Waxy House when we get back. I shall get permission from Fanny and I shall have it searched.'

Dolly weighed it up. 'Do any good, do you think? And which case – which crime – will you be working on? Alicia Ellendale, Arthur Doby, or the spectre of Waxy House?' She was sorry when she had said this because it sounded like a joke, and she did not wish Charmian, in her present mood, to think she was being mocked. Added to which, Dolly was deadly serious.

Charmian had her answer ready. 'Perhaps the lot, and don't laugh at me.'

'Well, I wasn't, but I would like to know the answer.'

They drove on in silence. Running into Windsor with the castle in view, Charmian said: 'Tear it to bits, if I have to.'

'Fanny will like that.'

Pushing from her mind thoughts of all the blue files on her desk demanding her attention, Charmian said: 'I wonder where Fanny is at the moment?' She looked at her watch. 'Only mid-afternoon.'

'Probably playing cards with her three friends.'

In fact, Fanny was at home playing dummy whist with only two of her friends, Ethel and Paulina, because Dorie was working.

'What she calls work,' Ethel said, laying out the cards. 'Just standing in front of a camera and holding out her hands.'

'She has got lovely hands.' Paulina reached out for her cards. 'And she earns a lot of money by it.'

Dorie was doing a commercial for a new hand cream.

Ethel turned her attention to Fanny. 'You don't look your best today, Fan, and I don't think you've had your mind on your game either.'

'Haven't had the cards, have I?'

'Never stopped you playing a good hand before.'

'She's had a bad night,' pleaded Paulina. 'Didn't you, Fan, love?'

'Yes, and so did Charmian Daniels.' There was satisfaction in Fanny's voice. 'Now she believes me when I say it's an unquiet house.' She looked at her cards.

'Lucky at cards, unlucky at love... I ought to look around me, there must be someone out there longing to embrace me.'

'You'd know, Fanny dear, if anyone would,' observed Ethel.

'I'll ignore that, Ethel, as we all know your love life was severely limited. If not non-existent,' she finished in an audible whisper.

'Oh, come on, you two,' said Paulina. 'Cards, please, not bitchiness...'

For a moment or two they played in companionable silence. The bickering meant nothing but gave pleasure to all parties. Paulina joined in when the right tart line came to her lips, and Dorie would always quote Noël Coward... 'So quotable, dears, and always so right.'

'I'm thinking of calling on my old friends Winnie and Birdie for advice and help,' said Fanny, when the trick was over. She had lost, so lovers look out. Old she might be, the toss of her head said, but didn't Catherine the Great go on having lovers till she died?

Birdie Peacock and Winifred Eagle were spinster ladies, living not far away, in a companionship that had caused many eyebrows to be raised. Gossip and speculation being spiced when Birdie was seen dancing naked round a tree in their back garden as she greeted the spring equinox. They were reputed to be very good at spells to promote well-being, excellent at talking to animals, patchy at predicting the future, and hopeless at forecasting the weather. On the whole, they were a much-loved local phenomenon. Up there with the Queen, Royal Day at Ascot, and the Windsor Festival.

'Those old witches,' said Ethel.

'They are good women.' Fanny was clear about this. 'On the side of goodness. I shall consult.'

'It'll cost,' said Ethel.

It was known that Birdie and Winifred did not give their services free, and although they always said that the money went to animal charities, people did wonder.

'I've spoken to them already,' said Fanny, 'on the telephone. I spoke to Birdie, who consulted Winifred, who said: Raise the temperature, the Devil cannot survive in the heat ... Wonder what she meant by that?'

'Keep out of the deep freeze,' said Ethel with a laugh. 'Your play.'

They played with happy concentration, breaking only for tea and cake, a sacred ceremony which they always honoured. This comfortable moment was broken by a telephone call for Fanny.

'Charmian? Hello, dear.' Fanny covered the telephone and turned to her friends. 'Pour the tea, Ethel, I won't be long, and Paulie, dear, you cut the chocolate cake ...'

'Fanny, I want your permission to go into Waxy House and search it from top to bottom.'

Fanny wasn't sure if she liked that. 'I'm not really the owner yet, dear. I don't know if it's for me to say.'

'I've spoken to Mr Grange, the solicitor dealing with the will, and he tells me that probate is through and Waxy House is all yours. It is all yours, Fanny, and you can give me permission.'

'What would you be looking for?'

'Just giving the house a look over, Fanny. You must

agree that what happened last night merits it. To try to find out who was in there.'

Fanny muttered something about spectral forces not having feet.

Charmian had no intention of telling Fanny that Arthur Doby had been a coin collector and possibly the source of the sovereign which they had found in Waxy House. But the murder was something Fanny had to be told; she would read it in the newspapers or see it on the television news, in any case.

She felt herself pregnant with heavy news of which she must deliver herself without alarming Fanny too much.

'I have to tell you, Fanny, and this is in confidence, that the coach driver, Arthur Doby, the driver of the coach that brought Alicia Ellendale to Windsor, has been found dead.'

'Lord, Lord, you don't suspect him of having any connection with Waxy House? Surely he can't be haunting it?'

'No, Fanny, I don't think he'd stray so far from London.'

'How did he die?' And when Charmian remained silent, Fanny answered herself. 'He was killed. Murdered. How?'

'It'll be in all the papers; wait until then. Besides, I don't know much yet myself.'

But you know more than you are saying, Fanny thought with her usual shrewdness. 'Is it connected with Alicia being missing, dead too, I suppose?'

'It may be, I can't say more than that. Not at the

moment. But I have your permission to search the house?'

'I suppose so. But I must think about it. I shall want to know more.'

'You shall, Fanny, in due course.'

Fanny put the telephone down. A ghost in her house was one thing; you could be interested, diverted, possibly in profit, from a ghost. But a search by the police was another thing. This would not improve the value of her property.

She returned to her friends, who had been drinking tea, eating chocolate cake and listening to every word.

'Pour me a cup, Ethel, please, and I'll have a slice of cake.' She cast a beady eye at the chocolate sponge. 'If you've left me any.'

'Plenty.' Paulina cut a generous slice. 'Here, on your favourite plate.' It was a small, round plate of fine china decorated with brightly coloured birds. Fanny said, and perhaps believed, that it was Meissen. 'She kept you talking. Bad news.'

Fanny frowned. 'She wants to search Waxy House. I couldn't say no. But I haven't agreed yet. I'll need to think.'

'I told you it would do you no good bringing her in,' said Ethel, over a mouthful of cake.

'No, you didn't.'

'Well, we won't argue. What was the other thing? There was something else, wasn't there?'

'The driver of the bus, the coach, that brought Alicia from London to Windsor, to the coach station at College Green. He's been found dead.'

Ethel put down her cup and Paulina stopped half-way through a mouthful of cake; this was better food and drink.

'My goodness. Murdered or suicide?'

'Accident, perhaps,' said Paulina, reluctant to think so.

'Charmian wouldn't say, but I don't believe it was an accident.'

'Suicide or murder, then.'

'She said it would be in the papers ... But this is in confidence, mind. And about the search. Keep it quiet, please. Mr Grange knows, so Charmian says. She seems to have got in touch with him. It should have been me first, but he won't say anything.'

But Mr Grange was already on the telephone to his friend, the accountant Bertie Bacon in Leopold Row.

'There's going to be a search of Waxy House. By the police. I thought you'd be interested.'

'I am. Do you know why?'

'No, but I don't like the sound of it. There was something said about antique coins, a sort of probing.'

'Ah,' said Mr Bacon thoughtfully. 'I took an interest myself once. Not for some time, though.'

'Well, there it is. I thought I'd just mention it. It is my duty to advise Miss Fanfairly to give consent.'

'You couldn't do anything else.'

'No. She hasn't yet agreed formally, which will be necessary. But I think I'll ask to be present ... as her representative.'

'Good idea. I've been worried about that house for some time, you know I have, and wondering if I ought to say anything. But you don't like to drop anyone into it.'

'No. Well, it's out of our hands now. But this is in confidence, you understand, just to you.'

'Of course, of course.'

But Angela Bishop, uneasy about her grandfather, had picked up a bit of the conversation. In the evening she would question Edward Underlyne and although he would look serious and say he could not talk about professional matters, he would in the end tell her all he knew.

In confidence, of course.

Meanwhile, Mr Bacon, after some thought and headscratching, said: 'Just out for a few minutes, Angela.' And he walked down the street to talk to the computer wizard, Harry Aden.

He told him that the house next door was going to be searched. And was he still a member of the Numismatic Society?

Harry Aden said no, he wasn't, he never had been, although he knew about it and he'd be glad if it would be remembered he was not and never had been a member, and thanks for the news about the other.

Then he sat at his screen and, pressing the right buttons, was soon able to read the local police computer screen and then, with what he picked up there, to concentrate on the Metropolitan CID and see what he could learn about the death of the man Doby.

Should he talk to his architect neighbour? he asked himself. Maybe, maybe. All this was confidential, and he would have to think about it.

THE WOMAN WHO WAS NOT THERE

He always had to remember Fenwick's wife. He never forgot her.

Frank Felyx had no computer screen to read, but he still had a few friends in the Windsor outfit, and in no time at all he knew as much as anyone of what was going on.

And he knew that now Doby was killed (and his friendly informant had given him a broad hint that he had better have a good story about his movements), then he was back as a suspect for the death of Alicia.

In fact the only suspect. And they did not yet have Alicia's body.

By nightfall Charmian had received a first report from the CID team dealing with Doby's death.

She was not surprised to learn that he had not long been dead when she had discovered him, or to know that he had died from a massive loss of blood. You could smell the blood in that room. Nor was it unexpected to learn that the forensic evidence suggested he had not struggled. Or not much. Taken unawares, they thought.

But she was surprised that the neighbour next door had said that she had seen a woman calling on the house early that morning and that the woman had a bad limp.

No, worse. More of a hop, skip and a jump with the help of a stout stick.

Part Two

The Woman Who Was There

Chapter Eight

Thursday

Evidence, on tape, delivered to Charmian Daniels, Head of SRADIC, in Windsor:

This is the evidence of Jean Barley, widow, aged fifty-eight, living at number five, Draper Street:

    I live next door to where the killing took place. Number five, as numbers go that way, is near the top of street, with a good view of it all. I live on the top-floor front. Since I am disabled, I sit at the window a good deal, just looking out and waiting for things to happen.

    No, I cannot move without help. My home help comes in twice a day, to get me up and put me to bed. Meals on Wheels gives me my dinner, Yes, I have got a wheelchair in which I can be wheeled around to the bathroom but I cannot get into it on my own... Well, as to what you are suggesting, I have to wait. You learn to manage. Anyway, I'm not allowed to drink much, and believe me sitting around all day is constipating to say the least, so the trouble is all the other way.

    Yes, I do read a good deal. I was a librarian before my troubles, but I keep an eye on the road. Not much gets past me. For instance, I saw you arrive, Sergeant, and I think you slipped in the mud and fell over. That patch of pavement always seems to be perilous.

You swore, too, if I'm not mistaken. Yes, I notice things.

This morning I was sitting at the window, I had had my breakfast and I was reading *The Times* and listening to the radio.

Yes, indeed, as well as looking out of the window I can do three things at once.

It was after ten-thirty. I can tell from the radio programme I was listening to – it is a programme for women and always starts at that hour. You can find it in the radio programme in the paper if you wish to check. The programme was about abortion and the rights of women: it very often is. You believe me, right.

It was the last item before the news on the hour, so it would be about ten to eleven. In the morning, of course in the morning. Do you think I don't know night from day? I know you have to check and be careful, but this is ridiculous. In fact, I think you're doing it on purpose to throw me.

I looked out of the window to see a taxi drawing up, and this woman getting out.

Long black dress, long full coat over that, and a scarf over the head . . . No, it didn't look odd, they all dress like that now. No, I couldn't see her face.

But I could see the way she walked . . . hopped, really, dragging herself along, poor soul. With a walking stick, too.

And she went in next door. No, I didn't see her leave, because my niece came in then and various personal matters were attended to.

No, my niece saw nothing, but you can ask her. I'll give you her address: Mrs Armstrong, three Chancellor Road,

THE WOMAN WHO WAS NOT THERE

Lewisham, and it's very good of her to come as often as she does because it's quite a bus ride. I pay, of course.

Yes, the woman in black could summon another taxi, there's a rank not far away, and she may have had a mobile phone, many people do have. And anyway, there's a telephone box not many yards down the road.

That is what I saw. I swear it.

A comment added on the tape by the Sergeant: WPC Mary Carter was with me at this interview, and both of us believed the witness. She seemed an accurate and honest observer. Mary says she knows her and it is well known that she sees everything.

A real turn-up this, isn't it?

Chapter Nine

Thursday and Onwards

Charmian set up her plans like a military operation. She asked Drimwade to provide her with a search party and equipment. It might be necessary to lay on strong lighting, so she would also need an electrician with his gear. Distantly she felt she could hear a cross Superintendent Drimwade gnashing his teeth and complaining about the expenditure. They would have to negotiate the budget, sharing it between them, always difficult.

And she told Rewley she would want him there. Mr Grange, Fanny's solicitor, had requested that he should attend, and Fanny took it for granted that she should. Dolly was to stay in the office and receive and collate such news as should come through. It was sparse at the moment. She could not say she was being kept in the dark, but there was a feeling of things being held back.

To Dolly, Charmian said: 'Find out how she got to the house.'

'Well, we know it was a taxi. No news in that.'

'They must know more by now. Where the taxi came from, where the passenger was picked up. They must have got the driver by now. Make them say. I get a whiff of obstruction in the air.'

THE WOMAN WHO WAS NOT THERE

Can obstruction smell? Dolly asked herself, but early next morning she did what the boss wanted. Amos and Jane were out of the office, dealing with all those cases that Charmian had, for the moment, put aside. They were biding their time, hoping to pull in a big result (say on the Ambrodine Fraud case) so that they could say to Charmian, look what we did while you were otherwise occupied.

Dolly was on the telephone early in the morning, well before nine o'clock, trying to contact Sergeant Edwards. After some difficulty – where *was* he? – she got him.

She recognized his cheerful, give-nothing-away style.

Oh yes, they'd interviewed the taxi driver. As a matter of fact, he'd done so himself. The man had come forward. What he had to say was simple: he had picked up the passenger at New Cross Gate station. Having just dropped a fare there, he was glad to pick up another at the unlikely spot.

Dolly was thoughtful. 'Did he wait and take her back?'

'No, another bloke got that job. He sounded pleased.'

'Why?' asked Dolly.

'The first driver said there was a stink in the cab . . . Like someone dying in slow time.'

'Quite a description.'

'He was that sort of chap. Some cab drivers get that way, it's life on the road that does it.'

'And what about the return trip?'

'We haven't traced that driver yet, but we will. It's early days.'

'Try harder,' said Dolly; she was beginning to like the sergeant.

'Come up and help me. My guess is that she rang from the box down the road and got the local car hire . . . The number's in the box.'

'Haven't you asked?'

'Of course. They're asking their drivers as they log in—'

'They keep records of calls, I presume.'

'Not as carefully as they ought to,' he said regretfully. 'Come up and have a word . . . Of course, it might not be them. There's another outfit used a lot round here with a base at Waterloo. Now meet me there; we can attack them together and then we can have a meal. There's a couple of nice little eating places I know.'

'Let me know when you have a result,' said Dolly with a laugh, putting down the telephone.

'Will do, a pleasure . . . And you'll let me know if you have any useful thoughts about the coin collection business.' He got it in quick before she rang off.

So he had noticed, Dolly thought. Clever bugger. She might go and have a meal if the opportunity arose. He seemed interesting and her life felt very empty at the moment.

And she had to admit that if the London end was being canny with information about the murder of Doby, she and Charmian had kept their tongues quiet too.

Mostly Charmian, she told herself; her responsibility.

THE WOMAN WHO WAS NOT THERE

Late morning, still busy when the telephone rang, she felt like ignoring it; but, ever dutiful, she picked it up. She had had a bad cold for days now and she was sneezing as she did so. For a second or so her sneezes kept time with the telephone rings. 'Hello. Inspector Barstow,' she said, her voice husky.

Fanny was not an early riser, as most of her friends knew, so she was surprised but not displeased to be called to the telephone at an hour that felt like dawn to her. In fact it was between eight and nine o'clock. Definitely dawn time to her.

Her landlady banged on her door and said there was a call for her, and to hurry on down, please.

Fanny had no telephone in her room, so any calls received or made had to go through the more-or-less public telephone in the hall downstairs. There was a box and you were trusted to pay for your calls ... Fanny was very honest. She had made up her mind that when she sold Waxy House, then she would buy herself a mobile phone. She fancied the idea of lying in bed making a call – most of her life had been centred on bed, and she saw no reason to change her ways.

She thought it was Mr Grange. She knew he wanted to see her and she had an appointment. She guessed he got up early; businessmen did, didn't they?

'Hello ... Oh, is that you, Frank? I didn't recognize you at first.'

Frank said he wondered if she would come to have breakfast with him. He wanted to talk, something he had to tell her.

'Oh, can't you do it now, Frank? You do sound bad...'

No, he wasn't ill, a bit upset, perhaps, he had had some bad news...

Neither of them mentioned the death of Arthur Doby of which Fanny was aware but preferred to ignore.

'The Peacock Hotel? Yes, OK, then.' The Peacock was a luxury hotel into which Fanny rarely ventured. 'Just give me time to get dressed.'

It was raining hard when she emerged. She held up her umbrella, put her head down into the nasty wind that was whipping up, and turned towards the Peacock. She was planning her breakfast. Orange juice, coffee and cream, an omelette, perhaps; she had heard the Peacock did great omelettes, and then a croissant or two. Fanny liked her food.

She stepped along happily. She liked Frank, even if she didn't always trust him. You couldn't trust a policeman, could you? And he was certainly behaving oddly. But she had learnt to be open minded about men: you had to take them as you found them, and take what was offered. Even if it was only breakfast.

She turned the corner, past the big supermarket, which was just opening for the day, crossed its car park and went past the narrow alley next to it.

The Peacock was very close, she could see the roof.

As she got to the opening of the alley a hand was clamped over her mouth and she was pulled backwards into the dark passage.

Her umbrella fell away as Fanny struggled. She

kicked with her feet, twisting and pushing, desperate to get free or at least get a look at her attacker.

'No breakfast for you today, Fanny,' murmured a voice. 'You'll be a bloody corpse lying here in the alley. Better to have done it in the house, but beggars couldn't be choosers.'

Fanny kicked hard with her high-heeled shoes.

'Bitch,' came the murmur in her ear, 'but now comes the knife.'

Mr Grange and Charmian waited for Fanny in Grange's office. They waited; Fanny was late.

She was very late.

Presently, it came to them that she was too late.

Edward Underlyne, who had been working outside, brought in coffee. Sexism was not accepted in the Grange office; the staff made the coffee and carried it around on a strict rota. The only person exempt was Grange himself – sexism was not allowed but concession was made to ownership. Mr Grange was the senior partner. Indeed, the only active partner. The others, T. Grange and B. Grange, were either sleeping or dead. W. H. (William Harry) Grange was the one who counted.

Edward handed Charmian her cup of coffee and offered her sugar, which she refused but with a smile. He was a good-looking lad and he knew it; he was used to getting smiles from ladies of all ages. He thought she was attractive and smiled back, but he would have done that anyway, being a polite boy. He knew who she was, because Angela had talked about her. He wondered if he ought to tell her that Angela was very worried about her grandfather, Frank Felyx, who seemed to be drinking too much and eating too little. But he didn't speak. Not really the occasion.

Presently he was back. 'Telephone call for you, Miss Daniels.' He knew she was Her Ladyship, but he also knew not to call her Lady Kent, since she did not use the title professionally.

Charmian was surprised. 'For me? Here?'

William Grange pushed forward his own telephone. 'You can take it here, or private elsewhere.'

'I'll take it here.' She grabbed the receiver. Grange gave Edward a nod. 'Switch it through.'

It was Dolly Barstow, with a short, quick message. 'Fanny Fanfairly has been found with stab wounds in an alley just off the town centre. She's in the Slough Road Hospital and her condition is poor.'

'Who found her?'

'A postman taking a short cut home after his morning delivery. Otherwise she might be dead already. She's lost a lot of blood.'

'Thanks, Dolly. I'll get round there.' Charmian looked at Mr Grange. Better take him too – there might be a need for a last will and testament.

Alicia Ellendale, Arthur Doby, and now Fanny. This looked like being one death too many.

Except that perhaps Alicia was not dead after all.

Fanny lay quietly in the intensive care unit of the Slough Road Hospital.

The hospital was a large brick building which had

been built as a workhouse by Victorian philanthropists. It had been constructed solidly and it would have cost more to knock it down than it had done to reconstruct the inside. It had been cleaned, repainted and new wards had been added. Recently it had received a great deal of expensive new equipment, but its past was not forgotten by the locals, who did not like it as much as they should have done. The intensive care unit was highly rated within the profession.

Fanny was hooked up to various tubes; she was one among several others, equally quiet. Not the only casualty of life. She had her eyes closed but as Charmian came up to the bed, she opened them. Her lips parted as if she wished to say something, but nothing came out.

Charmian took her hand gently. 'All right, Fanny, don't try to talk. Don't do anything that you don't feel up to.' She turned towards the nurse who had come in with her.

'She may talk if she wants to. She's going to be all right. She lost a lot of blood but we're making that up.' The nurse, a very young woman but professionally cool and gentle, smiled down at Fanny. 'Responding nicely.'

It's the response that pleases her so, was Charmian's reaction. A good patient is a successful patient, one who responds as expected. Nothing personal.

'Fanny,' she said, 'who did this to you?'

There was no answer, so she tried again. 'Is there anything you can tell me? Anything you saw, anything that would help us identify your attacker?'

Murderer, she almost said, except that it seemed

Fanny was not about to die. Granted that she was an old lady and that the wounds and loss of blood might not enhance her chances of long life, but she was not going to die today.

The local detective sitting by her bed, a gentle, dark-haired girl who had introduced herself to Charmian as Detective Peggy Lane, said that they thought the attacker might have been frightened away by something or someone before finishing off his job.

Fanny kept her eyes closed for a few seconds, then she opened them slowly. 'Don't know, smell, stink, tried to see ... Black. Looked like ...' She seemed to gather strength. 'A black abbess.' She closed her eyes, and a faint smile moved her lips. 'I was one myself once.'

'And what that meant,' Charmian said afterwards, 'I don't know.'

'An abbess was a woman who ran a brothel; or a procuress,' said Dolly Barstow briskly. 'A piece of eighteenth-century slang. Not in current use, as far as I know. Fanny's a special case, of course.'

'Yes. She was one.'

The two women were talking in Charmian's office. Charmian had made coffee, which they were drinking. Rewley was out on other business but had left a message saying he had heard of the attack on Fanny, and where did that leave the search on Waxy House? At the moment, Charmian did not know, but she had sent most of the men away, leaving one man on duty and the search to start again the next day.

'I don't suppose she called herself an abbess. But she appears to be using the idiom. I suppose she knew what she was saying?'

'She was only half-conscious, but she seemed rational enough, and she wanted me to know. Why black?'

'Fits in with the visitor who probably killed Doby,' Dolly pointed out. 'She was wearing black. And walking badly.'

Charmian hesitated. 'The Met you were talking to haven't picked up any more information about this visitor, presumed killer?'

'One thing more: they've located a second taxi driver who picked up a person meeting the description and took the fare to Waterloo railway station. He too complained about the smell left behind in his cab.'

'Smell?'

'Oh yes, you won't have got that report yet. I heard it on the telephone and I think it's now been faxed to you. The first cab driver said the limping fare left a stink in his cab ... The second said it was like dead fish.'

Charmian said slowly: 'It links up with something Fanny said.'

'About the limp?'

'No, I don't think she got a chance to see the feet ... No, she muttered something about a smell.'

'You'll have to speak to her again.'

'I will do as soon as I'm allowed. She's not too well, you know. I can't bully her.'

'Poor Fanny,' said Dolly. 'I can't bear to think of her alone in that hospital.'

'You're hardly alone,' said Charmian absently. 'Crowded with nurses and doctors taking tests all the time. Not to mention the other patients.'

She took her cup of coffee to the window. Outside it had ceased raining and a few patches of blue had appeared in the sky. 'We've got to find Alicia Ellendale.'

'I get the impression,' said Dolly, 'that although the South London boys are being very professional in their investigation of the murder of Doby, they really think it's up to us.'

'Alicia Ellendale, where are you?' said Charmian from the window.

She turned as a fax came fussing through. Dolly stood up.

'Might be the latest from the dashing sergeant.'

Charmian gave her sharp look. Dashing, indeed. 'Get it, will you?'

When the several pages had come through and the machine had gone quiet, Dolly picked up the sheets; she skimmed through them. 'Yes, it's what South London is giving us. May not be all they've got, and it's more or less what you know already . . . Wait a minute . . . here's one last item.' She raised her head. 'Here it comes: it's about the second cab driver, the one who delivered his fare to Waterloo. The fare used a stick getting out of the cab, but the driver didn't feel inclined to help, having taken a dislike to her.' She looked at Charmian. 'On account of the smell, I daresay. We really must work on what that smell was . . . He stopped and checked on the inside of the cab at the first possible moment, and found that the fare had dropped a rail ticket on the floor. He forgot to tell the sergeant at first. The sergeant thinks he was hoping to sell his story to the press but, being disappointed, was willing to pass the information on.'

'The ticket?' queried Charmian, with impatience. 'Pass it here, please.'

'Return ticket to Windsor,' said Dolly. 'Over to us, isn't it?'

'As soon as Fanny is allowed visitors, I'll be in there,' said Charmian. 'I suppose Drimwade will have one of his men there, but I want to be the first to ask questions.'

It was some time since she had undertaken the first questioning of a victim of attempted murder, but she was determined to do so now.

Twenty-four hours passed, hours in which the enquiry into the death of Arthur Doby and the hunt for Alicia Ellendale proceeded without producing results.

But Fanny was recovering speedily. She was moved out of the intensive care unit into a private room. She lay back on her pillows, astonishingly cheerful. As she said, a good blood transfusion does wonders for you; look at Dracula.

And she was certainly not alone. Visitors flowed in as soon as they were allowed. The police, of course, were there all the time, in the silent presence of one or other of the officers of Superintendent Drimwade.

Ethel and Paulina together with Dorie got in first. Insisted on it as close friends, and with Dorie putting on her act of being a welcome guest at the Castle, they managed it with an ease that surprised even them.

Dorie said if knowing HM (which she did, she wanted them to recognize) hadn't worked, she was prepared to put on her medical manner and say she was head of surgery at St Bede's. She had played that in a soap and knew the manner to a T.

They came with flowers and fruit, and although Fanny could not eat easily and the scent of the flowers was too strong for her, she was delighted to see them.

Since she could not talk much either, they did it for her.

'My filming was a big success,' said Dorie, who always thought her own news was what counted. 'I shall get a nice lot of residuals.'

'Hands, was it?' asked Ethel, who regarded it as her duty to cut Dorie down to size every so often.

'No, no, I was presenting the product. A new little luxury ... You'll see it on the screens. It's going to be test-marketed in the south.'

Paulina patted Fanny's hand. It was she who had brought the flowers, and Ethel the fruit. 'You poor thing, so awful for you. You shouldn't go out at night on your own.'

'It wasn't night, it was morning,' Fanny managed with difficulty. The knife had missed all vital organs, but her throat ached.

'And so much violence around.'

Eagerly they discussed the killing of the coach driver, Arthur Doby, in his home in London.

'And, of course, it must connect with that poor woman whose foot was found ... now where is she, one has to ask?'

'And now you,' said Ethel.

THE WOMAN WHO WAS NOT THERE

'We don't know that the person who attacked Fanny is the one who got Alicia Ellendale.' Paulina put her hand protectively on Fanny's.

'And who probably killed Doby,' went on Ethel. 'Likely though, isn't it? Mind you, the police don't seem to be getting anywhere. Thick lot.'

The policewoman sitting tactfully in the corner moved her feet at this bit of conversation, but they ignored her.

'We must stir them up,' said Dorie.

'You'd better work your connection with the Queen.'

'No, Ethel.' Dorie was dignified. She knew that Ethel was envious of her continuing career, even if the new product soon to burst open the southern counties was only a new form of chocolate drinking powder. Anyway, not babies' nappies or tampons, Dorie told herself, I've haven't touched those. She ignored the secret little voice inside her which said and too old, far too old. 'I meant Fanny's friend, Charmian Daniels.'

'She's been nothing but trouble,' said Ethel. 'I reckon she brought this on our poor Fanny.'

'She's Lady Kent,' answered Dorie, who always knew these things. 'Her husband is a knight.' Not a peer, not a baronet, nothing inherited (life peers were better avoided), but meritorious all the same.

A nurse put her head round the door. 'You'll have to go now, ladies, the doctor's coming.'

Which was a lie, but she knew how much her patient could stand. And Dorie was well known to her by sight. An exhaustion all round, that one, she thought. And the fat one who had brought oranges and apples, which she might have guessed the poor patient could not eat. Only Paulina with flowers passed her private good-for-a-patient test.

Mr Grange did not call at the hospital in person, but after talking on the telephone to Charmian, and consulting the hospital authorities (he liked things done with due formality and the correct protocol), he sent Edward Underlyne to the ward with a bunch of flowers, and the orders just to enquire.

Edward soon discovered that Fanny was now in a small room, but he thought his orders held good so he handed the flowers over to the nurse on duty.

'How is Miss Fanfairly?'

'Recovering well... Needs rest, of course. I'll put the flowers in water for you. She has another lovely bunch but these are even nicer.'

'Thank you.' Edward had chosen them himself: pink roses, which he thought neither bridal nor funereal, not blood red.

'Popular lady.'

'She has a lot of friends.' And an enemy as well, Edward thought, but did not say so. He wondered where Frank fitted into this picture and if he had visited Fanny. Probably not, he thought.

On his way out, he passed a couple of men walking towards Fanny's room. They walked side by side like a pair of yoked but badly matched oxen. He did not know their names but thought he knew the faces.

THE WOMAN WHO WAS NOT THERE

This surprising pair of visitors came from Leopold Walk. Having discovered that Fanny was allowed visitors, Harry Aden and Christopher Fenwick came together. Christopher had flowers and Harry a bowl of fruit.

Fanny was propped up on her pillows, resting quietly but feeling the pain of the wound in her throat. The stitches were stiffening in the skin and underneath both muscle and ligaments were bruised.

They introduced themselves, but Fanny already knew the names if not the faces. The fat one and the thin one, she decided, Laurel and Hardy, except she did not feel they were comedians. The thin one had an interesting face, lined and drawn, but the fat one, although he looked jovial and good humoured, also gave the impression of forces underneath which might not be so jolly.

No doubt her state made her sensitive.

The fat one led the conversation. 'We thought we ought to offer you our sympathy and good wishes as neighbours, or neighbours-to-be. You will be living in Waxy House?'

He really wants me there, thought Fanny, always responsive to a man who showed interest. 'I'm thinking about it,' she said, sniffing the flowers. Her nose puckered; she was sensitive about smells now as well, no doubt about it.

'I don't know if I'll be living in it. You know what it was? A kind of a brothel. It may not be the right house to live in.'

'Decisions are difficult,' said Chris Fenwick. He had a deep, husky voice, not without appeal. 'Life's difficult.'

'Dying is worse,' said Fanny with decision. Having come so close, she felt she was an expert on the subject.

'Your voice is bad today, Chris,' said Harry Aden.

'Just a virus, I don't think I'll infect you, Miss Fanfairly.' Chris Fenwick bent towards her politely. 'Don't want to lose our new neighbour before we've really got her.'

'As I said, I haven't decided whether to live there or not. It needs thinking about. I may sell.'

'You'd buy, wouldn't you, Harry?'

'On the spot. I want to expand.' Harry Aden smiled. He might have gone on to say more but Fenwick interrupted him.

'Think twice about his offer, Miss Fanfairly,' said Chris Fenwick. 'Do a bit of bargaining . . . I could help you there.' He said it with humour, but Harry did not smile back. Chris did not want him to have Waxy House, he could tell.

They don't like each other, Fanny thought, not really. She closed her eyes gently, indicating it had been kind of them to come but it was time they went. 'Most kind,' she murmured, feeling regal.

The door opened slowly and Charmian Daniels put her head round it.

'Nurse said I could come in to talk to you, Fanny. But I'm afraid it means turning you two out.'

Fanny held out her hand. 'Come in, come in.' She gave the two men another smile but did not offer to introduce them. Her professional life had trained her never to name men. Especially to a policeman. In any

THE WOMAN WHO WAS NOT THERE

case – her experience again – the police always seemed to know any names that mattered.

Charmian did not disappoint her. 'Ah, gentlemen, an embassy from Leopold Walk.'

'Just a courtesy call to a new neighbour.' Harry Aden was smiling at her, his plump face divided into two by the width of it, which made you realize he had a large mouth which showed his teeth and might not be as friendly as one hoped. 'Got to get back... My mother will have lunch ready.'

'Oh, mothers,' said Fanny agreeably. 'I remember my mother fussing if I was late for a meal. Late for anything.' She hardly remembered her mother, in fact, and had left home as soon as she could, but she always agreed with men; it was part of the job. She smiled at Chris Fenwick.

'Oh, he doesn't have to bother,' said Harry Aden. He gave a little laugh. 'His wife's away.'

'On holiday?' asked Fanny with false sympathy. She was a stupid wife, though, to leave this one. He was attractive and interested in women, she could tell that. Her skin, bones and other more intimate parts of her anatomy informed her of his attractions.

'Business,' obliged Chris.

'Busy woman,' said Harry Aden. He made for the door.

'What did they want?' Charmian asked as the door closed behind them.

'They came to see me,' said Fanny, not unproud.

'That too, but what else.'

Fanny examined her hands, looked at her nails, which had been broken in the attack as she had defended herself. 'I'll need a manicure. My clothes, too . . . all blood . . . Will I get damages, compensation?'

'In time. Yes.'

'Can I sue my attacker?'

'We have to find him first. Or her.'

'A strong her,' said Fanny with some feeling.

'Some women are strong.'

'I've strong legs, good thighs, one of my assets, and I've always known what to do with them.' She gave a throaty laugh.

'Come on now, Fanny.'

'Saved me. I could fight with me legs. Women can.'

It was probably true, Charmian thought.

'I think they came to see if I would sell Waxy House. That and other reasons,' she added thoughtfully. 'I'm sensitive at the moment, always have been, but something like this makes you more sensitive. And I felt that they wanted to ask questions. They might have done so if you hadn't appeared.'

It was possible they had got wind of the plan to search Waxy House. Charmian had always regarded Mr Grange as a leaky vessel.

'Funny pair,' said Fanny. 'Coming together like that, one fat, one thin. They didn't seem to have much in common.'

They had a woman in common – Charmian remembered Frank Felyx's gossip – Fenwick's wife.

'How much do you remember of what happened? I suppose you've had the local CID in asking questions.'

The policewoman in the corner, who had sat stolidly through the Leopold Walk invasion, looked at Charmian.

THE WOMAN WHO WAS NOT THERE

'Leave us alone for a few minutes, please,' said Charmian.

The girl hesitated, then left. 'I'll be outside.'

'They haven't asked any questions,' said Fanny.

'I bet they've wanted to.'

'I'm supposed to be too ill.'

'And are you?'

'I've got a rotten headache, and it hurts where the knife went in, but I feel more myself today.'

Tough old bird, Charmian thought. At death's door one day and flirting with two men the next.

'I don't remember much at all, except what I said . . . Black, you know. Dressed in black.'

'A woman? You used the word abbess.'

'Did I?' Fanny frowned. 'I wasn't myself . . .' She shook her head. 'I don't know why I said that now. I must have sensed something.'

Charmian said: 'What were you doing out at that hour? Not your usual style.'

Fanny kept quiet. 'I dunno,' she said vaguely. 'Can't remember now. It's gone.'

'Come on, Fanny. Drimwade is going to press you on that. Your landlady says you had a telephone call. Does that have anything to do with getting you out so early?'

'Oh . . .' Fanny took as deep a breath as her wound allowed. 'OK, all right . . . the call was from Frank.'

'Frank Felyx?'

'I don't know any other Frank,' said Fanny irritably. 'He said he wanted to talk to me. Or did he say he had something to tell me? Now that I honestly can't remember.'

'I can ask him,' said Charmian. She sneezed.

'Your cold is bad. I could tell you'd got one the minute you came in.'

'Forget my cold. About Frank. You can't remember what he wanted. No? Has he ever asked you to breakfast before?'

'No,' Fanny gave her infectious giggle. 'We have never breakfasted before, and this was to be at the Peacock. Not like Frank to splash his money around.'

'No, it isn't.' Charmian recalled the man who had moved his custom from one pub to another because of the noise. She sat back. 'All right. Let's leave it there. Just get in touch with me if you do remember anything.'

'And you'll come running?'

'Yes, I will, you old wretch.' She bent to kiss Fanny's cheek.

'You didn't bring any flowers or fruit.'

'You seem to have plenty.' She moved towards the door. 'What would you like?'

Fanny said: 'Not fruit or flowers . . . Biscuits, please, the food is awful here.'

As Charmian got to the door, Fanny said: 'I can smell that smell . . . I reckon it's got stuck in my nose. Not biscuits, please, but a spray of that nice violet scent . . .'

'Right,' said Charmian, smiling to herself as she walked away. Fanny was still Fanny.

Then, before the policewoman could get herself back in, but when she could hear what was said: 'Fanny, have I your permission to go over Waxy House?'

THE WOMAN WHO WAS NOT THERE

'Yes, all right. But take care.'

'All the care in the world. I'll get Mr Grange to send you the papers round to sign.'

She looked at the WPC, who had heard every word and could bear witness if necessary that Fanny had given permission.

'Blow the papers,' she said to herself as she drove down the Slough Road. 'I'm going into that house.'

But she wanted a word with Frank Felyx first.

Chapter Ten

Into the weekend and after

Frank Felyx had created a sanctum for himself that suited his way of life: inside his house it was muddled, cosy and warm, a one-man nest, an igloo, protecting him not from snow but from the world.

His garden he neglected; he had never cared for gardening, although while his wife was alive he had weeded and mowed to please her, but now he regarded it as no more than a place to bury the odd dead bird or cat.

Any drinking he did now he did at home – he was avoiding the pubs. He knew well that he was an object of suspicion. He might have made away with Alicia Ellendale; he had been named by her and consequently had been questioned and had seen his house searched. The garden had been inspected: they'd have that dug over soon, he told himself sardonically.

Only they can't quite make out how I could have done it, seeing there are no witnesses and no forensics for them to lay their hands on.

Haven't got Alicia's body, either. That worried them.

At one time, the chief suspect had been either him or Arthur Doby: the shoe found in the refuse bin at the coach car park had pointed the way to Doby. Although Frank knew well that there was a school of thought among his former mates that believed he had planted it there. Certainly now Doby was dead, murdered, that left him on his own, in pole position, and under suspicion for Doby's murder.

Although he was leading a solitary life there was still the telephone, and he had his contacts – he knew about Doby and about Fanny. But his contacts were becoming increasingly reluctant to talk to him and he knew that too.

He sat in his comfortable old armchair by a window which could have done with a wash and let a few names roll round his mind:

Phyllis Adams, Jane Fish, Mary Grey, Kathleen Mace, working girls all; probably not a real name among them.

It was raining again, which he was glad about because it gave him an excuse for not going out; he thought he had a cold coming on, a lot of them about. He had probably handed it on to the detective who had come calling on him that morning.

A former colleague had come round questioning. Not that he called it that. Just dropped in for a drink with a pal. Oh, yes, and with Drimwade's keen permission to do so. His old colleague was Sergeant Jacaponi, whose father had come from Italy as a PO and had decided to stay. He had married an English girl from Berkshire, and together they had produced several children (of whom the sergeant was the eldest) and a successful dog- and cat-meat factory.

Jacaponi had the air of being uneasy at the task

set him and had brought with him a bottle of whisky. He knew that when Frank was out of temper with him, and it had happened, he had called him the Cats' Meat Man.

'Didn't get a chance to come to your leaving bash, so I thought it was time I looked in.'

'No. You were on holiday.'

'Yes, I went with the old man to see his family, or what's left of it, in Milan.'

Get out of him where he was the morning that Doby was killed. I want to handle this quietly, Drimwade had said.

'Haven't seen you around lately,' Bill Jacaponi began.

'You've been away.' Frank allowed himself a slight smile. Think I don't know what you're after, the smile said. And then he relented because in his way and on the right day he had liked the sergeant whom he now regretted having labelled the Cats' Meat Man (a name which he knew had joyfully been taken up by his colleagues in the CID). 'To be honest, I haven't been out much at all.' He thought of saying he had been doing a bit of gardening, but a quick look through the window suggested that the lie would be a bad idea. 'Felt like staying quiet. I read a lot.' That was true at least. Then he relented entirely. 'Let's open that bottle. My favourite malt.'

'I know.' Which is why I chose it, he said to himself. Jacaponi watched Frank bustle out to the kitchen; he could hear the tap running and guessed he was washing the glasses. Well, that was something, because judging by the look of the sitting room not much else was cleaned.

Ponged a bit, too. Bill Jacaponi himself usually rubbed his face and hands with an Italian toilet water, which was, he guessed, why he had got his unlovely nickname. It was the British male striking back.

Frank opened the bottle and poured them each a substantial draught. If the sergeant thought the drink would loosen his tongue then he was mistaken.

'No, haven't been out except to do a bit of food shopping and not much of that. I'm running a bit short.' He grinned, showing well-browned teeth.

'Not good to be too much on your own,' tried Jacaponi, almost able to predict the answer he would get.

'I like my own company. My grand-daughter drops in occasionally, and Fanny Fanfairly, but I don't think I've seen anyone for the last few days.'

Not admitting going out, but no one here to admit to seeing him, translated the sergeant to himself. It looked as though that was all the news he would be taking back to Superintendent Drimwade.

Good news, bad news, how could he tell?

He left soon afterwards, realizing that if he stayed on they would finish the bottle of whisky between them, and though he guessed his head was as strong as Frank's he had no desire to put it to the test.

'You won't be my last visitor today,' said Frank, pouring himself another whisky.

'No?' Jacaponi guessed he meant a visit from the investigating team, and no friendly bottle of whisky would be next. Even one from the Met. He himself had had a call from Sergeant Edwards.

'No.' Frank smiled, 'and I don't mean my granddaughter and her boyfriend... He's a lawyer, you know. I might find that useful.'

If Jacaponi had hung around, instead of reporting straight back to Drimwade that he had got nowhere – if he had stayed and watched the street, he would have seen the expected caller arrive.

'Knew you'd be here,' said Frank. 'Had one visitor asking questions already, now you, and you won't be the last.'

Charmian saw the bottle of whisky on the table, smelt it on his breath and drew at least one accurate conclusion.

'You've been drinking.'

'Yes, the bottle was a present. Can I pour you one?' Never forget you are a gentleman, Frank, or nearly one. Might have been one once with a better education and a bit more money.

'No, thank you, and I'm going to make you some coffee. I think you could do with it. I want to talk to you.'

'I wouldn't mind some coffee,' he said meekly enough, aware that the whisky had got to his legs and would get to his mouth if he wasn't careful. And with speech and Charmian Daniels you had to be careful. 'I wouldn't mind a slice of toast if you can find the bread.'

I must be drunk, he told himself, giving orders to her, Lady this and Chief of that. He closed his eyes and leant back against the cushion.

When he opened them Charmian was sitting there, looking at him. A cup of coffee and a slice of buttered toast were on the table beside him. Chilling nicely, by the look of them.

'Had much sleep lately?' she asked, and her voice did not sound friendly.

He pulled himself together. 'I wasn't up in London killing Doby, if that's what you mean.'

'You know about his death?'

'I've got my channels. I may be retired, I may be under suspicion for I don't know what, but I've still got my contacts.'

'I'm aware of that, Frank. I never thought you were totally ignorant of what was going on.'

'Not totally innocent, either. I can see that in your face. And it's what you're here to find out.'

'Maybe, maybe not.'

'After all my years in the force, I think I might have been trusted more.'

'Let me put it like this, Frank: Alicia Ellendale, whose relationship with a certain division of the Met in South London seems to have been close, has disappeared after saying she was coming to Windsor to see you.'

'She never came near me,' Frank said in a thick voice. 'And it was only Doby's word she ever meant to.'

Charmian moved on smoothly: 'She has never been seen again after leaving the coach from London. She was last sighted walking into the town. Later, a severed foot in a shoe was found near the river. Both were identified as Alicia's. So alive or dead, she was without a foot or a shoe. Later still, that other shoe of hers turned up in a litter bin at the coach station. Mysteriously.'

'It's all a mystery.'

'It's fair to say that you came under suspicion at first, then the needle swung towards the coach driver, Arthur Doby.'

'It's a gamble, isn't it?' said Frank. 'Roulette.'

'Of course, he was under suspicion from the first. Bound to be. But no real evidence against him, except he was not perhaps the nicest of men ... You were, Frank, or judged to be.'

'Good old honest, reliable Frank. That was it, wasn't it?'

'You've lost that merit badge, Frank. Perhaps you were not as nice and straightforward as you seemed. Or perhaps you've changed since you retired.'

'Is that a question?' he asked, leaning forward.

'I don't think you've changed, but we all of us have different faces for different people and different times, so I think we're just seeing a different face. I think you might remember, Frank, that people have to be prepared for change. You didn't do that, you just let us see suddenly that underneath that reasonable police officer was a man with the usual emotions and not all of them nice.'

Frank did not answer. So what? he thought.

'I'm not blaming you, just explaining that some of the trouble you're in is because you didn't prepare us to see what you are.'

'And what am I?'

'A man with a strong sex drive who had a lot of dealings with people like Fanny and Alicia and knew them better than you ever let on.'

'Could be. I don't deny it. I like Fanny, the old bitch. How is she, by the way?'

'Getting on all right. Although a good attempt was made to kill her. She thought she was invited out to breakfast with you.'

'Have I ever invited Fanny out to breakfast?'

'You must have offered invitations in the past for her to believe in this one. She certainly thought it was you.' Charmian was watching his face. Little expression showed, except anger.

'One or two, perhaps. My sex life, such as it is or was, is nothing to do with you, ma'am. And as for inviting Fanny to breakfast, I didn't.'

The telephone rang in the hall.

'Answer it.'

'I'm not going to, let it ring.'

Charmian got up and went into the hall. He did not try to stop her. 'Hello,' she said into the phone. There was a sound of breathing and then the line went dead.

Frank looked at her with a kind of triumph. 'Wrong number?'

'Wrong person answering. I'll find out who's keeping you so well supplied with information before I'm done. I'm warning you, Frank.'

'A man must have a few friends.'

She still couldn't make up her mind whether she thought he was guilty or not. He seemed to keep one step ahead of her, like a dancer. You are a cleverer man than I ever thought you, Frank, she decided.

I'm getting to be a bad judge of character, she told herself, a skill I had always prided myself on. Perhaps

I never was as good as I thought. I'm also irritable and depressed. Something else I used not to be. Or not to show.

Perhaps Frank and I are both showing different faces – the ones underneath, the ones we kept hidden. I'll be honest with him, just for this once. Not playing games.

'I came round here, Frank, to make up my mind if it was you who telephoned Fanny, attacked her, and if it was you who killed Doby.'

'And I bet you're still wondering.'

'I think I am, Frank. That's a warning.'

'So I'm still up there – chief suspect?'

'I'm afraid so. The only one at the moment.'

He took a long drink of the coffee that must now be quite cold. Then he wiped his mouth free of the moustache of coffee that had rimmed his upper lip and leaned forward, hands planted on his knees.

'But my contacts tell me that the view now is that it looks as though the person who killed Doby was a woman.'

He leaned back in triumph, there was no mistaking it.

Charmian did not answer directly. 'I have to find Alicia,' she said. 'Alive or dead, she must be found. And when she is found, she'll tell us something, whether about you or someone else.'

'And about the other missing women?' he said. Phyllis, Jane, Mary and Kathleen. 'Don't forget them.'

'I don't forget them,' said Charmian.

'All working girls and you know what that means.'

'Yes. Sex.'

'There's a lot of it about.'

'You don't have to tell that to someone who's seen Waxy House.'

'Yeah, and not all of it waxy and dead,' said Frank sardonically.

'Yes, you've already said that Harry Aden is in love with Mrs Fenwick. How does she feel?'

'No idea. I never asked. I know about him because he told me: I could love that woman, he said.'

'Only could.'

'That's what makes it important,' said Frank. 'If you can't see that you can't see anything.' He leaned back in his chair, closing his eyes. 'Go away now, please. You can come back and arrest me any time. I won't run away.' He sounded weary. 'Not much good at running anywhere these days.'

Charmian stood up. 'I'll see myself out.'

'You do that.' He opened an eye. 'And if you run across my grand-daughter, tell her not to come to see me. I want to be left alone.'

At the door she turned back. 'Frank, one last question: What did you mean in the pub when you said Mrs Fenwick had a funny sense of humour?'

He stirred in his chair. 'Oh, perhaps nothing . . . I saw her one day in Brown and Frasers, that big store in Slough, and she was buying a great long black raincoat.'

'Not shiny?' asked Charmian.

'No, dull, heavy, and I said to her what's that for? And she laughed and said, "For when I am a man." '

'Are you saying she was bisexual?'

'Not saying anything. You asked, she said and I told, that's it.'

'Or that she was the woman in black who killed Doby and attacked Fanny?'

'You're saying it, not me. You put the question and I answered, and that's it.'

He closed his eyes again. 'Pull the door behind you.'

Charmian sat in her car outside his house, thinking over their conversation. Frank had come up with a neat idea and put it across well. There must be a search of Waxy House, and it had to be thorough. She would need twenty-four hours.

'I gave him the chance,' she said to Rewley, in her office on Monday, 'and he took it. Before my eyes, another woman in black, who might be bisexual, appeared. We have two candidates now: Alicia, not dead, but damaged and limping, and Caroline Fenwick. I haven't met her, by the way. She's said to be away on a work project.'

Charmian had had a busy twenty-four hours, and more.

They were seated together in Charmian's office, in the half-hour before the search of Waxy House was to start, going over such new reports of Doby's death as had come in. 'Nothing much there,' Rewley had said. 'Let's send Dolly up there again to work on the sergeant. She gets on well with him and may pick up what they are really thinking.' He pushed the papers – faxes, copies of telephone calls, a medical report saying that Doby had a bad heart and would have died quickly

THE WOMAN WHO WAS NOT THERE

– away from him across the table. 'These are just routine stuff.'

'It was always going to be us in trouble,' said Charmian. 'That's why we got the job. They don't like the idea that Alicia Ellendale may turn out to be not lost and dead but out there killing. Can't say I blame them.'

'It's unlikely in fact, though, isn't it?'

Their eyes met. 'Yes,' said Charmian. 'Too many hard facts against it . . . Let's be hard and name them. Shall I start? One, the medical opinion was that the foot found in the shoe in Windsor was from a corpse.'

Rewley nodded: 'And that person was identified by the malformed toe as Alicia.'

'Exactly right. And then, if by some medical muddle, it turned out that Alicia was not dead when the foot was hacked off . . . roughly, it appears – then she must have needed help. Somewhere there would have to be a hospital or a doctor who treated her.'

'I guessed we ought to investigate that possibility,' said Rewley thoughtfully. 'And I sent out a DC to do it. So far nothing . . . Do you expect it? I'd be surprised, I think, if anything came back.'

Charmian realized that she liked working with him because he was so intelligent and often said what she was just thinking. She went on: 'I don't believe even hopping and with a stick a woman with a newly severed foot could have got around. You'd need practice for that. You can bet that the London mob have worked all that out and are just waiting to see if we have.'

'So the woman in black was a phantom?'

'Not quite that, but not what she seemed to be. It was a fascinating picture, I quite enjoyed it, it was like being in a Wilkie Collins novel, or Dickens – he could have managed it.'

Rewley summed it up. 'What you are saying is that the murderer was someone dressed up, acting a part.' He was frowning. 'Has to be someone who knows about Alicia and her foot . . .'

'As her killer would. And Frank, under suspicion himself, has produced a name: Mrs Caroline Fenwick, and she comes with the strong hint that she is bisexual.'

'Male – female, it's a sort of tightrope, anyway, isn't it?' said Rewley. 'Still, it will be interesting to meet Mrs Fenwick.'

'Surely her husband will know where she is.' Charmian stood up. 'Let's get down to Leopold Walk. They'll be waiting for us now.'

Amos Elliot and Jane Gibson were in the outer office as Charmian and Rewley came through. They were standing at Jane's desk, head bent over a folder of documents and photographs.

Amos turned towards Charmian and Rewley. 'Tricky case, this one. Been sent on to us from Addlewade.'

Addlewade was a new estate beyond Merrywick, built about five years previously to provide luxury homes for those rich enough to afford several garages for large cars, a mooring on the river Thames, and an annex for 'staff'. Unfortunately the estate had been finished just as money had run out. Or at least had been severely depressed. Many of the houses lay empty.

But nature does not love emptiness and the houses became occupied by unexpected residents.

THE WOMAN WHO WAS NOT THERE

'There was this chap,' said Amos, 'must have just wandered in, meaning to doss down for the night, but he took too much of his favourite drug mixture, a fairly lethal cocktail by all accounts, and went to sleep for ever. Straight case of death by misadventure... But look at this photograph.'

He held out a photograph of a human arm and hand. The arm was small, thin, and could have been that of a woman; the hand was tiny and well kept, with ring marks on it.

'He called himself Fraser Markey, but he wasn't a man but a woman. And look at the hand again... The fingers are all torn; the thumb's missing. So is it murder?'

'No,' said Rewley at once. 'I know about this case... Not murder, a fox got in and did the chewing.'

'Can't catch you,' said Amos. 'Indeed the fox, unidentified so far, did the chewing, but the woman was dead then. The legal view is that she was shut in the house by the local security guard, who had locked the house after leaving it open for motives of his own. There are signs she-he tried to get out. So where does that leave the security guard, and did he take her in there in the first place? We're required to do some work on the case.'

'How did the fox get in and then out?' asked Charmian.

'That too requires an answer. A murky case,' said Amos with satisfaction. 'I'll let you know what we come up with. And if you want to know why Jane is in on this, it's because she thinks she may have been at school with the dead woman.'

Jane said nothing but continued to pick up the photographs to study.

'I didn't really enjoy that,' said Rewley as they drove away. 'It's just a game to those two, like chess.'

'Not to Jane, I saw her face. But still to Amos.' Both of them would change, though, toughen, until what they did would become not a game or an intellectual exercise but a job. Whether that was a good thing or a bad thing, Charmian could not decide.

It did not happen to the very best officers, of whom Rewley was one, who never forgot that the dead were human. Whether she too was such a one, Charmian was never sure. Perhaps it was not one of those things you could judge of yourself.

Charmian drove as speedily as she could through the crowded town traffic, and took the turn into Leopold Walk. Two police cars and a plain van lined the kerb.

Angela had been staring down the road as the first of the police cars had arrived about half an hour previously. She was still watching when Charmian drove up.

'Do come away from that window.' The senior clerk, Freda Langley, regarded it as her job to keep order in the office. 'Old Bacon will complain.'

'It's the police.'

Angela had been alerted by Edward Underlyne that the delayed search of Waxy House was about to start. He had telephoned earlier that morning, providing

THE WOMAN WHO WAS NOT THERE

another cause for comment by Freda, who pointed out that personal calls were not encouraged in office hours.

'Any minute now,' Edward had said. 'Although I don't know what they think to find in that empty old house.'

'The house isn't empty.' Angela gave a shudder. 'Not empty at all . . . You know we said that this is a Michael Gilbert story? We were wrong: it's Edgar Allan Poe.' She began to make soft gulping noises.

'Come on, old thing,' Edward said. 'Don't go hysterical on me, it's just a game, I thought you'd be interested.'

In the office Freda took the telephone away from Angela. She did not speak to Edward. Let him sweat. But she had got Angela a drink of water and stood over her until she stopped gasping.

Now the girl was at it again.

Mr Bacon came into the room. 'What's that noise?' He looked at Angela. 'Is she all right? What's up?'

'She's a mite disturbed at the idea of the police in the house at the end of the road.' Freda allowed herself this quiet understatement.

'Oh, ah.' He went to the window to look out. 'I can see the police there.' He stood contemplating the scene: several uniformed officers and a tall man with fair hair whom he recognized as Superintendent Drimwade. 'Wonder what he's doing there?' He watched Charmian getting out of her car. He knew her, did not know the man with her, but if he was with Charmian Daniels then he had to be important. 'Don't upset yourself, my dear,' he said to Angela, although knowing as he did (and most of Windsor too) of the rumours about Frank, he was not surprised she was emotional. And then, you never knew with young women – sex, young men, menstrual problems, they all came into it, he told himself sagely. 'Take the rest of the day off. Take a walk, have a rest.' He headed back to his own room, to his telephone which was already ringing and his clients, always fussing. He gave one last look at Angela. Pretty girl, he liked pretty girls. Don't worry, kid, Frank's no murderer. Sex, yes. Killing, no. And he toddled off – he had put on weight lately – back to his own personal confusion.

Freda patted Angela's arm. 'He means well. You go home if you want to. I can manage.' A slight tinge of self-pity coloured her words. Old Bacon could afford to be generous; he wouldn't worry how she would get on, all that paperwork to do and the dodgy WP.

Angela drank some more water. 'No, I'm better now. It was very silly and emotional of me. I ought to know better. But I've been worried over Grandpa.'

'I know.' Freda had been given an account of some of Angela's worries; the girl might be making too much of her grandfather's behaviour, but perhaps not. There was certainly talk in the town which she had heard but not contributed to; she had her own brand of loyalty. In any case, better perhaps not to say you knew the grandchild of a killer. 'Let's have a cup of coffee, and then we can get back to work.' A cup of something was always her remedy.

Charmian got out of her car to find the tall figure of Drimwade approaching.

'Thought I'd come round to see how things went.' He looked at the end of the road where a few onlookers, attracted by the police presence, were already gathering. 'Have to put some barriers up or we'll have the crowds upon us. Not to mention the press.'

Not here yet, thought Charmian with some relief. Drimwade was right, though, they would come.

'Have to get those cars moved,' went on Drimwade, nodding towards two cars in residents' parking bays. 'We'll need that room.'

'Chris Fenwick and Harry Aden... I want to talk to them anyway.'

In a conversational way, Drimwade said: 'I sent young Bill Jacaponi round to Frank Felyx this morning to have a few words with him. Seemed a good idea.'

'I thought someone had been there. Called myself.'

'Guessed you would do. Was he any help?'

'No.'

'Jacaponi didn't get much out of him either... Here comes one of the men you want to talk to.'

Harry Aden had walked out of his front door and was coming towards them. 'My car is going to get blocked in. What's going on?'

Charmian did not answer. 'If you move your car round the corner it will be clear.'

'No parking, yellow lines.'

'I'll see you don't get clamped.'

Harry Aden went to his car, muttering that if she

could control the traffic warden then she was pretty clever because no one else could.

'Come back when you've done. I want to talk to you,' Charmian called after him.

While she waited she watched what was going on. Waxy House was being invaded. The door was wide open, as a police team moved in.

Chris Fenwick touched her arm, and she swung round. 'Ah, you should move your car while you can...'

'What is all this?'

'You can see.' She did not feel inclined to say more. 'But I'd like to talk to you.'

Harry Aden stumped back, not pleased. 'Well, what is it? Here I am, talking.'

'You can see that Waxy House is being searched. I wondered if you had ever noticed any person going into the house?'

'No.' Short and blunt.

She shook her head. 'Ever heard noises, sounds of people there?'

'Never noticed a thing.'

'Would you call yourself someone who doesn't notice things? Are you an unobservant person, Mr Aden?'

'When I'm working we could have an earthquake and I wouldn't notice.'

Charmian considered him: in a blocking mood and better left for the time being. 'I'll come back to you later; you may remember something.'

Chris Fenwick came up, car keys jangling in his

hand. 'So?' He stared back at Waxy House. 'What's happening in there?'

'Just an investigation we're engaged in,' said Charmian blandly.

'A non-answer if ever I heard one.'

Harry Aden said: 'She's been asking me if I ever heard anyone in Waxy House . . . or noises? Funny noises, did you say?' He put his head on one side. 'How funny?' He nodded towards Fenwick. 'Why don't you ask him?'

'I shall do.' Charmian turned briefly to look at Fenwick, who was showing his teeth in a half-smile, and not an attractive one. 'But you, Mr Aden, live nearer to the house.'

'And more chance of noticing anything dubious?'

'Something like that.'

Chris Fenwick said tartly: 'Does Miss Fanfairly know about this?'

Charmian nodded. 'Of course she does. This search is at her request.' Not quite true, but it would do.

'And is it connected with the attack on her?'

'I can't answer that. Have you noticed any activity in Waxy House?'

'It's supposed to be empty. Are you saying it's not?'

Charmian did not answer.

'Another non-answer,' said Fenwick. 'Anyway, I never notice anything when I'm working.'

'Mr Aden says the same.'

'It's called concentration.'

'What about your wife? Would she have noticed anything? I'd like to talk to her too.'

Fenwick said abruptly: 'She's working abroad at the moment.'

'Do you expect her back soon?'

'I don't know.'

'Perhaps I could have her address?'

Fenwick started to move away. 'She travels around.'

Charmian blocked his way. 'Come on now, Mr Fenwick. You can do better than that.'

'I can refuse to answer.'

Charmian stood her ground. 'You would do better to talk.'

Fenwick's face changed. 'All right, all right . . . She's left me.'

'So where is she?'

Fenwick swung towards Harry Aden: 'Ask him.'

There was a moment of silence, as before a duel. Then Harry Aden said: 'She didn't come to me; I wish she had, I love her. But she isn't with me.'

Before Charmian could speak, she became aware of a small disturbance in Waxy House, a noise, police officers coming out, going up to Drimwade. Other men moving across towards the house from the police van. Then Drimwade coming across to her.

'Bit of trouble in there.' He ignored the two men, still squaring up to each other as if direct fight could not be far away, and went on to Charmian: 'Electricity expert trying to give us a bit more light, put his leg through a floorboard . . . Rotten, he says, and fungi and God knows what growing thick under the floorboards. Nasty.' Then he drew Charmian away from Chris Fenwick and Harry Aden. 'What's up with them?'

THE WOMAN WHO WAS NOT THERE

'They're quarrelling over Fenwick's wife,' said Charmian shortly.

'I see. Well . . . this isn't for their ears. The man who put his leg through the floorboards . . . He's found some bones.'

Chapter Eleven

All days are working days

Charmian walked towards Waxy House beside Drimwade. She would have liked to pursue her conversation with the other two men; they were upset, angry, and you always got more out of angry men than they wanted you to know. It might not be important, but you could never tell. As her old university tutor had once said to her, concerning historical evidence: it was all grist to her mill.

She followed Drimwade into the narrow hall of Waxy House where the strange, familiar mixture of smells rose up to greet her. A new element had been added with the arrival of the police team, who smelt of aftershave and tobacco smoke. She frowned, trying to remember and assess the old smell.

The ancient carpet in the hall, probably laid before the *Titanic* sank, had been pulled up, revealing the wooden planks underneath. These were cleaner than she had expected, but dark with damp in patches.

'Dangerous house.' The electricity specialist looked down at his right leg where the white uniform was speckled with blood.

'It certainly is that,' agreed Charmian.

'I had one board up and moved back and my leg went right through.'

'You should have been more careful.' Drimwade was not very sympathetic.

'That's just it: I am. But this house has its teeth out.' He looked down at the floor. 'And you can see that for yourself. One victim.'

In the light of a torch, the electricity being off, they stared down at the small collection of bones. A tiny head, bent over a curving backbone, the legs drawn up.

Tiny as a cat, but not a cat. It was human.

'A baby,' said Drimwade. 'Poor little soul.' He had seen more than one dead baby, but it always moved him.

'The child has been here a long while,' said Charmian.

'It'll hold us up, but I don't think it'll throw any light on contemporary problems.' And for that matter, he said to himself, I'm not a hundred per cent clear why you want to go through this house.

Charmian hardly knew herself, but there was an inner conviction that always came back whenever she questioned what she was doing, that Waxy House had its part to play in the disappearance of Alicia Ellendale and the death of Arthur Doby. And probably also of those other missing ladies: Phyllis Adams, Jane Fish, Mary Grey and Kathleen Mace. But the baby, she guessed, had been laid to rest before any one of them was born.

She looked away, sharp memories of the case she had been involved with a year before, when her god-daughter had died. This truly was a horrible house, able to tap into one's private miseries.

'I don't think this discovery has anything to do with what I'm interested in,' she said.

'And that is?' asked Drimwade, gently, quietly.

'I think you've guessed that for yourself: the disappearance of Alicia Ellendale and the murder of Arthur Doby.'

'We've had mixed stories about the Doby murder,' said Drimwade. 'Limping ladies dressed in black . . . I take it you don't accept that?'

'Not entirely.'

'It's an interesting idea, though.' Drimwade had an amused alertness at the back of his eyes that made her wonder: what does he know that I don't?

'I read in the report that Doby was a coin collector.'

'There were coins found in his flat,' said Charmian, wondering what was coming.

'I expect you know we investigated a coin-collecting society in Hounslow . . . Several men from Windsor and Merrywick and a few from Cheasey.' He paused. 'In fact, it was the Cheasey contingent that first caused suspicion . . . After all, you don't expect a Cheaseyite to be a coin collector, except to steal and spend, of course.'

So what's he going to tell me next? Charmian asked herself.

'It was investigated because we thought it was a cover for a porn group . . . Frank Felyx was on the investigating team.'

'I'd like to see that report,' Charmian said grimly. She looked towards Rewley, who had come out of the house to join them. 'Get it for me, please, as soon as possible.'

He nodded. 'Sure.' He gave Superintendent Drimwade an interested look. Clever bugger, he thought, he's been keeping this back.

'I wasn't here myself at the time,' went on Drimwade, 'so I don't remember the details. But it would be well worth your looking at it.'

That means he remembers it and knows there's a crucial fact in it. Coins, he thought, a coin ring. Who'd have thought it?

'How did the coin society come to be suspected?' he asked.

'Ah, that's interesting in itself,' said Drimwade. 'No one talked about the society, which seemed harmless enough. I mean who suspects numismatists of evildoing? But one of the club, society, or whatever, was involved in a car crash and documents were found in his car. Lists of names, all assumed but one or two men from Cheasey were identified and people started to wonder. I understand that's how it came about,' he ended carefully. 'But as I say, I was not here myself.'

'So what happened?'

'Those who could be identified – were arrested.'

'How long ago was this?'

'About eight years.'

Charmian said: 'I was doing a course in London about then . . . Still, I ought to have caught up with it.'

In a careful voice, Drimwade said: 'At least one of the men convicted had what might be called high connections. Nothing was hushed up, but everything was low profile, if you get me . . . Couldn't do it now, but then you just about could.'

Charmian said: 'The search of the building will be held up by the discovery of the bones. I'll get away, there's plenty I can be doing, then I'll come back.'

'I'll tell you what I'm going to do as well,' said Drimwade. 'I'm going to check the movements and alibis of all members of the numismatists' club, all those that we can find, for the time of Doby's death.'

'Good idea,' said Charmian. 'And run over the people who work in Leopold Walk as well. There aren't too many so it shouldn't be a great task.'

In the car Rewley said: 'Do you think he knows who we'll turn up in this report?'

'No. He's too good a policeman for that. But he thinks there's someone there we might identify.'

Rewley made a doubtful noise, indicating that Drimwade's expression suggested he knew more than he was saying.

'He's got the sort of face that looks as if he knows something,' said Charmian thoughtfully. Been an asset in his career. 'It's his eyebrows and that thin smile. I don't believe he'll get much from checking the alibis of the survivors of the coin-collecting club, even if they can be found. I don't think that's the way forward.' Routine police work had to be done or questions would be asked. 'And he's going to include Leopold Walk. I want to ginger them up a bit there.'

Rewley studied her face, but it gave nothing away.

'Traffic's heavy, isn't it?' she said, and he took that as a final mark on their conversation.

As she drove on she remembered that she needed

food for the cat again, and the dog too if he was coming home from his stay with Birdie Peacock and Winifred Eagle. He was with them most days when she had to be out. There was food but more was needed. A husband ought to do that sort of shopping, she mused, turning left in the main shopping street, but Humphrey, although willing in theory, was never home enough to shop. He must shop for his clothes, she supposed, choose shirts and shoes but she never saw him at it. Probably he had a large wardrobe which rarely needed replenishing.

There was a supermarket which she patronized in this street but parking was impossible; cars lined the street on either side. Then a small car loaded with a woman, two dogs and a big box of shopping moved out.

'I'm going to stop here,' she told Rewley. 'I need some cat food. Will you wait here, or come in?' Then she saw his expression. 'No, you go back to Waxy House. You want to, don't you? I'll get hold of the report on the coin collectors of Merrywick.' Dolly could do it. The days were gone when she went running around on such errands herself. She half regretted it, you learnt a lot on errands like that.

'I do want to go back, I want to be on the spot.'

'You can walk from here. Call me when they get back to searching the house. I want to be there.'

She soon finished her shopping, carefully selecting the tins of food that the cat liked and which the dog would also consent to eat. On occasion the cat ate dog food with no ill result. Fortunately, neither had learnt to read, although they knew the shape of the tins and the sound of them being opened.

She was making her way to the check-out desk, working out which queue it would be best to join, when she heard a commotion.

Running feet and voices raised.

Two boys were being led away by a security guard. She recognized one of them: it was Angus Cairns. That was not good, that was definitely not good, because surely this was the second time. She had seen this before here. Only that time he had got away.

She raised an eyebrow at the check-out girl. 'Oh,' said the girl, taking her money. 'If it's their first time and they haven't nicked too much the manager will give them both a ticking-off and tell them not to do it again. But we've had a lot of trouble lately, so he might threaten them with the police. He'll tell the parents too.'

Charmian walked out to her car. No, not good. She judged Dr Cairns not an easy or a forgiving parent.

She frowned. I must be getting old, she told herself. I'm more on the side of the child than the parent. Ten years ago I would have said wretched boy, poor father. Not now.

Dolly, of course, was out of the office. Amos was there, hunched over a pile of papers on his desk. 'She's gone to London, I think. She finished her work on that fraud case – you'll find the papers on your desk, I saw her put them there – and she said she'd be off to London to talk to the sergeant there. She thought she could get more out of him than he was passing along.'

But when Charmian told him about the report, he stood up, young and eager. 'I'll go, ma'am.'

Charmian got down to some of the other work that she had pushed aside for too long. She worked on, concentrating and, for a while, the disappearance of Alicia Ellendale and the murder of Arthur Doby receded into the middle distance.

When Amos came back he was smiling. 'I think I'd call that a well-read report,' he said, putting a brown file on her desk. 'Everyone who could invent a reason for having a look must have done so.'

Charmian opened the file. 'Yes, it does look well thumbed.'

'Breathed on with hot breath,' said Amos, 'and handled with sweaty fingers. I have to admit that I had quick look myself as I came over... It's the photographs.'

'Well, that's it for you for now,' and Charmian shooed him away. He went off, grinning. Amos was a good and very promising young officer, but sometimes she wanted to pat him on the head like a dog and say good boy. All the same, he had been with her for over two years now. Time soon to move on. He deserved promotion; it was her duty to see he was set on the path.

She was still bent over the file when Rewley walked in.

The photographs so diverting to her colleagues had not held her attention for long. She passed them over quietly to study what really interested her: the list of names and pseudonyms of those belonging to the club.

She looked up at Rewley, half abstracted: 'Well? Time to go?'

'Don't hurry. They're stuck. Pity those bones turned up in a way, as they complicate it all. Can't be ignored and must be dealt with according to the rules. No police surgeon. The one on call is held up with family problems. Drimwade is not pleased.'

'I know what the trouble is,' said Charmian. 'It's his boy, shoplifting. But if I have Dr Cairns aright he won't waste too long on tears and sympathy, he'll be along to Waxy House.' His work was where his heart was, not in family life.

Rewley stared over her shoulder. 'I see what you've got there . . .'

'Yes, look: two lists. First the names of those identified, assumed names in brackets, and, underneath, those whose disguise was never penetrated. Those who got away with it. I'm not interested in the first group,' said Charmian absently.

Rewley was, and he pointed to one name in the top list. 'I know that name, an old Cheasey name. Checkwinder, pseudonym: Cheater. He was that all right.'

Charmian ignored this. 'These are the names I'm interested in.' She pointed to the group of pseudonyms whose identity had never been established.

> J. Birthday
> T. Candleman
> S. Claus

THE WOMAN WHO WAS NOT THERE

She pointed to a name. 'I find that one illuminating. Surprising, too. Shows how mistaken one can be.'

'You less than most,' said Rewley, picking up the sheet and studying the names.

'Thanks. I hope the vote of confidence is justified.'

'Going to tell me what you think?'

'Later. I want to consider it. I may not be right.'

'Don't I remember that Frank Felyx called Harry Aden Daddy Christmas?'

Charmian tidied up the file, then locked it in a drawer. 'I'd like to keep that safe. Yes, I remember what Frank said. Not one of his better jokes, but descriptive. Aden is plump and can be quite jolly. It suits him.'

She stood up. 'I'm going round to Leopold Walk to see if I can hurry things up. Drimwade still there?'

'He was when I left. Drinking coffee in the van. He had just refused to be interviewed for the local TV news. Nothing to say yet, he told them.'

'Let's go.' Drimwade had pointed her in the direction of the names in the report on the coin society. Interesting, that; it might be that Drimwade himself was someone she had been wrong about.

They passed Amos in the outer office. He stood up as she went past and murmured, 'Ma'am.'

'Rewley.' They were just going to the car. 'Take Amos out for a drink when you have time and get it across to him that he need not call me ma'am all the time. Once a day or once a week will be enough. It makes me feel like the Queen and even she must get fed up with it.'

'He's a good chap.' Rewley liked Amos and, being

able to lipread, he had a better knowledge than Charmian of how Amos talked when he felt authority was elsewhere. Not that he had ever been critical of Charmian. Too sensible, too prudent, but one or two other colleagues had come in for some sharp comment.

'Very good and he ought to move on soon so as to keep up his career momentum. He must get experience outside of SRADIC.'

When they got to the car, Charmian gave him the keys. 'You drive, I want to think.'

She found herself thinking aloud: 'At first, when Alicia Ellendale – oh, I do dislike that name, it's so phoney – when she first disappeared, it put Frank under suspicion. Then the shoe turned up in the coach station and so I turned my mind to Arthur Doby . . . Is there anything from forensic on that shoe, by the way?'

'No, nothing. No fingerprints and no fibres or particles to match. The shoe is new and plastic.'

'Doby then got himself killed. And for a mad moment it looked as though Alicia might have done it . . .'

'Some character togged up in black and limping did do it.'

'Yes, so naturally, once I stopped thinking about a dead woman coming back or an undead one with one foot gone going into the kill, then I thought perhaps it was Frank dressed up.'

'Can't see that myself,' said Rewley. 'Frank may be many things, but I don't see him as a killer.'

'No, I agree. I think I agree, although I do feel he was a bit more into the porn side of the coin collectors than he admits. I don't say he was a member but once he found out about it, when he was asked to look into it, then he was interested, very interested indeed.'

'I can understand that,' said Rewley charitably. 'It's one of those things.'

'Then, and I don't know what to make of this, but when I visited Frank he suggested, quite cleverly, that Mrs Fenwick might be a bisexual killer who dressed herself in black.'

'Ask her, have a look at her.'

'So I will as soon as I get the chance. But meanwhile . . .' Charmian rubbed her head. 'I think I must be in a very suggestible state . . . Drimwade told me about this report and I could tell it was not an idle suggestion; he meant something. He meant that one of those names might be the killer. And one of those pseudonyms did start me thinking.'

'I know. I saw that.'

'You're a good listener, Rewley.'

'Gave me some ideas, too.'

Charmian hesitated. 'I won't ask you. May not match with mine, and I'll keep mine to myself until we see what Waxy House has to offer us.'

The afternoon had turned dark and rainy and the lights were on in the house. The electricians had trailed a cable across the pavement so that strong lighting was beamed inside the house and up the stairs.

Rewley found a spot to park the car further up the road and out of the light. 'If I believed in spooks I would wonder how they liked being floodlit.'

'The spirits in this house need more than artificial light to drive them out.'

Rewley looked at her in surprise. 'That's a thing to say.'

'Yes, I know. Not like me to go in for intuition. Well, logic is coming in too.'

Drimwade met them at the open door, where they could see into the hall, bright with light. The floor was up and a figure was kneeling by the hole.

'We're bogged down here for a bit,' said Drimwade. 'Doc has just arrived. He says the bones are so old he can't be sure if it's a baby or a monkey . . . Joke, not that he's in a jokey mood. It's a baby but it's been there too long to concern us; it seems no case for the coroner.'

'So what's happening now?'

'Now the lighting is fixed up, and that took some doing, the whole house is being photographed in case the dummies have to be moved.'

'They will have to be moved,' said Charmian crisply. She turned to Rewley. 'In the first place, they are interesting historically, and secondly, Fanny says she's thinking of opening the place as a museum, so she tells me.'

'Thought she was going to knock it down.'

'Changed her mind. She sees a hope of profit.'

Dr Cairns had risen from his knees. He was talking to one of the uniformed men in the hall.

'The doc is about finished. I know the signs. We'll be able to push on. He's brought the boy with him,' commented Drimwade to Charmian. 'Said it was that or chaining him to the bed post.'

'Where is he, then?'

THE WOMAN WHO WAS NOT THERE

'In the van. I left a WPC with him. She's giving him a cup of tea and a chocolate biscuit, if I know her.'

'May be what he needs, a bit of comfort,' said Charmian. 'He's the boy who found the shoe and started all this off.'

In a quiet voice, Drimwade said: 'I know that. And between finding that shoe with what was in it and having the doc for a dad, I don't altogether blame him for a bit of shoplifting . . . Know what he was taking? Shoes, trainers. I don't know if that's a symbol of something or not. Second go, too. The store said he'd tried once before, helped by a friend.'

Charmian turned to Rewley. 'You go into the house and start things up: I particularly want that big looking-glass on the landing looked at. I'm going to the van to talk to the boy.'

Angus and the woman police officer were sitting together by the open door of the van, staring out at the rain. Both held mugs, and, yes, there were chocolate biscuits.

The WPC stood up when she saw Charmian and took up her duties. 'Like a cup of tea, ma'am?'

'No, thank you, but I would like to talk to Angus.'

Angus turned nervously from woman to woman. 'It's all right, Angus,' said Charmian gently. She glanced towards the woman, who said at once: 'I could do with a breath of fresh air, if that's all right by you, ma'am?'

Angus watched her retreating back. 'She's nice. The police in the supermarket weren't as nice as her.' He put his head on one side. 'You know about it?'

'I know about it all. How's your father taking it?'

'Horrible,' said Angus with sad conviction.

'He'll calm down, I expect.' But she didn't believe it.

'Not him. He can't understand. He likes corpses; it's work to him. I hated finding...' He hesitated. 'What I found,' he said obliquely.

'Better to think about it clearly,' said Charmian. 'Face it out. We all have to.'

'It eats you up. Nibble, nibble, nibble.'

'Bite back.'

He laughed. A better sound, Charmian thought, than the shaky voice he had used. 'I'm frightened. That's why I wanted the shoes, to run with. So I could run and run if I had to.'

'Why steal them?'

'Dad wouldn't buy them,' he said simply. 'Just wouldn't. So Jaimie, my friend, said steal them. He steals everything.'

'I'd drop that friend.'

'You don't drop friends. And Jaimie's in trouble now; he's been caught so often before.'

Dropped himself off, Charmian thought. Just as well, really. 'What were you frightened of?' As if I didn't know.

'I think I saw who put the shoe where I found it...'

'Go on.'

'I didn't tell quite all the truth.' He stopped there.

'Tell it now,' instructed Charmian.

'I found the shoe because I knew it was there... It was there the day before. I was walking by the river, it was something I often did, on my own, or with my father, and my mother when she was with us... She's dead, you know. Father says she has gone away but I know she's really dead. It's just his way of putting it.

THE WOMAN WHO WAS NOT THERE

'I saw someone put the shoe into the river – not throw, just gently let it plop in. . . . I wondered what it was. It didn't sink, it got sort of stuck on a little raft of plants. I got it out, I thought it might be treasure.'

Charmian raised an eyebrow.

'Oh well, not treasure,' he amended. 'But I wanted to see what it was. When I saw, it didn't look nice, you know, kind of bloody and chewed. The rats hadn't had it, although they would have done, if I'd left it. I didn't know what to do. So I hid it. And then, next day, when I was out walking, Dad wasn't far away, I pretended to find it.'

'Thank you for telling me. I thought it might be something like that. So you saw who left the shoe?'

Angus nodded without speaking.

'And what did this person look like?'

'In black, all in black.'

And this was all Charmian could get him to say. 'Right, we'll leave it there, Angus, but I might want to talk to you later, in case you remember anything more.' She saw him flinch. 'Do you think this person saw you?'

He nodded.

'I understand why you're frightened and why you wanted to run. We all want to run sometimes, Angus.' She stood up, moving towards the door. Distantly, down the road, she saw Angie leaving Mr Bacon's office. 'I expect your father will want you now, Angus. He's probably ready to leave.'

Angus hung back. 'I don't want to be alone. Dad's got to be out tonight, he's on call.'

'He won't really chain you to the bed.'

He managed to smile. 'No, of course not. He thinks it's funny to joke like that. But I don't want to be on my own.'

Charmian put her hand on his shoulder. 'I would take you home myself, if I could. But I have an idea.'

Still keeping her hold on him, she stood outside the van as Angela approached. She knew Angela, and Angela knew her; they had met once in happier days in Frank's parlour.

She waited as the young woman came up. 'Hello, Angie.'

Angela, surprised and cautious, said hello back.

Charmian put her arm round Angus's shoulder protectively. 'If you're not doing something else this evening, Angela, could you look after Angus . . .? Let him come home with you? I'll see he's collected.' She looked down at Angus.

Angus and Angela had been eyeing each other with the caution and suspicion of two animals meeting for the first time. But Angela smiled first, and then Angus smiled back.

'Yes, please,' he said. 'But what about Dad?'

'I'll settle it with him.'

Angela asked, 'Do you know where I live?'

'I do.' Charmian had, in fact, been collecting a dossier on Frank and his family, just in case. She knew about Edward Underlyne. She had realized for some time that the chain of communication around Frank and Leopold Walk was quick and effective.

But she no longer feared Frank Felyx. She had other prey in mind. And Frank, in his devious way, had been useful.

'A lot's been happening here,' she said to Angela. 'I expect you noticed.'

'Couldn't miss it.'

'No. Well, thanks for what you're doing. It's Angus Cairns, by the way. And, Angus, this is Angela Bishop.'

'Miss Bishop.' Angus gave a little bow.

'Angela will do.' She held out her hand. 'Let's get walking.'

'Look after yourselves, both of you,' said Charmian. 'He's a good boy, and he writes poetry.'

They watched Charmian disappear into Waxy House, where she waved to them from the door. Angus saw his father in the recesses of the hall but decided to pretend that he had not.

When the two of them reached the flat where Edward was already cooking supper, Angela introduced Angus to him.

'He writes poetry,' she said. 'Angus, you can wash your hands and hang your coat up in my bedroom. Bathroom next door.'

Angus, who knew a dismissal when he heard one, prepared to disappear, but before he went there was something he must say, he was burning, bursting with the weight of it. He could have told Miss Daniels, but she had shelled information out of him as if he was ripe and this last, hard little nugget had refused to move. But it must move. Angela looked kind.

'Can I talk to you?'

'Yes, sure. After supper.' She turned the television set on. 'Here, after you've washed you can watch this. I'll call when supper is ready.'

Angus hesitated. 'Thank you,' he said.

'Where did you get him?' asked Edward over the fried onions. 'Risotto, Underlyne-style tonight, by the way.'

Angela explained. 'And Eddie, this isn't an Edgar Allan Poe story we're in, after all. No, it's Wilkie Collins: the Widow in Black.'

For she, like a lot of other people, had heard the rumours. But Edward had heard them too.

'No, Wilkie Collins is too matter of fact. There is something definitely ghoulie and ghostie about this business: I think it's more Sheridan Le Fanu.'

Chapter Twelve

Hours Now, Not Days

Charmian entered the hall where figures in silhouette against the harsh strong lights cast grotesque shadows, angular and twisted. Waxy House had never known such lighting in all its history: it was built for lamplight and the soft flicker of gas.

She saw Dr Cairns' sturdy silhouette grabbing his bag while muttering about collecting his son and getting away to another appointment. 'Done my bit. It's for the pathologist to take over now. Not much to work on, though, with that poor little bag of bones.'

Charmian interrupted him to let him know where Angus was. The reaction was not friendly. A huffing and puffing, she called it to herself.

She was unmoved. 'He needed company. You said yourself you have to be out.'

'I have a meeting to go to.'

'You can pick him up on your way home.'

Cairns muttered something about trouble, a shop and shoes. He sounded both angry and resentful. He was the injured party, his voice said, even if his actual words did not.

'And if he wanted shoes, running shoes, trainers, to run in, you might have to ask yourself why he wants to run,' said Charmian tartly. Beastly little man. He wasn't little in size but he was little in spirit. Still, being a parent, a single parent, was difficult, she had to recognize that. Not that he would admit as much. He probably thought if the boy said thank you and ate what was given him, then the father was a good father.

But to her surprise he stood outlined against the door, then muttered something resembling a thank you. It was only a mutter but it sounded grateful.

'Angus is a poet, you know,' she said. 'May be a good one, or he will be in time, and poets need special treatment.'

As he went out, Cairns turned and pressed her hand; she felt embarrassed, but pleased. She had done Angus a good turn. She only hoped that happiness, if it came his way, would not stop him writing poetry. Poets seemed to need the stigmata of pain.

She was so abstracted that she banged into Drimwade, who had been standing at the bottom of the stairs talking to Rewley, and, as she now realized, listening to every word she had said to Dr Cairns.

She took a deep breath and smelt the old smell of Waxy House that had so puzzled her on the night spent here with Fanny, that aroma of old decay with an overtone of dampness. Mould, it might be, but something else as well, it might almost be disinfectant. She sniffed again, trying to ignore the smell of tobacco smoke and work out the constituent parts.

She thought about that very smell . . . Surely there had not been a whiff of tobacco smoke on that disturbing night? Not there at first but silently seeping in. It needed thinking about.

THE WOMAN WHO WAS NOT THERE

'Nice to have the fresh air blowing through,' she said, noticing it was Drimwade who had been smoking, pushing the stub of his cigarette into a small tin box and looking guilty. 'No criticism of your cigarette,' she said. 'I used to smoke myself.'

'I know I shouldn't do it. Bad for the lungs, bad for the heart and ruins your sense of smell.' He looked around. 'Am I mistaken, or is there an unusual smell in this house?'

'Yes, I noticed it myself on other visits, even a bit stronger today.'

'Coming from under the floorboards, where they're up,' said Rewley tersely. 'You need good noses in this job.'

He was right, of course. Smells were important in this case, in which Doby's killer had smelt so strongly. Of fish, was it. Not a good idea to have a cold, like Sergeant Edwards in London. A passing thought about Dolly Barstow shot through her mind only to be pushed aside with amusement. The sergeant had fancied Dolly, and it might be that Dolly had a like feeling for the sergeant.

The first wax figure was carried out of the ground-floor dining room.

'We're bringing out the girls,' said a joking voice, followed by a loud voice commenting on the genital equipment of both male and female models, which was, it appeared, surprisingly detailed in its delineation, only visible when the clothes were lifted.

I must have averted my eyes, Charmian decided, I never noticed. Wonder if Fanny did. 'Be careful with those figures. They're valuable,' she ordered.

This was followed by an even coarser request from below not to knock off any of the sticking-out bits.

'Who's looking after these figures?' Charmian asked Drimwade. 'And where are they going?'

'I've got someone from Madame Tussaud's. Very interested, he is. Calls them of great historical interest. Apparently there were several such collections that he knows of, but this and one in Paris and another in Rome are the only surviving collections. He had read about this collection in memoirs and letters of the time but they were vague about where it was. So he was pleased to find out.'

So Fanny might make a go of a museum. 'I think more than a few locals knew.'

Drimwade was silent. He was one of those who had known, as was Frank Felyx; word got around. But obviously people in more sheltered circles like academia were slower to pick up place names.

'And the inhabitants of Leopold Walk knew,' she went on.

'They only work here, don't live here, but yes, I guess they knew. Stories get handed on. I'm surprised they didn't try to get in.'

This time it was Charmian who was silent. Did he know what he was saying? But he was both sharp and devious. He might be saying it on purpose to see how she reacted.

'I've been wondering that myself,' she said.

'You'd think the next-door neighbour, the computer chap, Mr Aden, would have wondered.'

'Of course, computer experts stay close to the screen in my experience.'

'I'd put Aden down as an inquisitive fellow.'

'So would I,' said Charmian. She realized that Drimwade was recalling the list of members of the coin collectors club. Did he knew that Frank Felyx's nickname for Aden was Daddy Christmas? He probably did. Frank might have been quite free with it. Free with a lot of odds and ends of information, she reminded herself; he kept popping in this little scrap and this little nugget.

Her eyes met Drimwade's in a silent communion so that she realized with a shock that he was thinking as she did.

From above came a crash. 'Oh, there goes that lovely. She's kicked over a chair, that's the trouble with being as stiff as a board.'

'Fancy her, do you?' called out another voice.

'Not me, no, like a bit more movement in the legs.'

Involuntarily, Charmian remembered Fanny's comment that she had always had strong legs; clearly good working equipment in her profession.

She was reminded of Bernard Shaw's play: *Mrs Warren's Profession*. Considered mighty shocking in his day but his first big success, which said something. It was still done today, but it no longer shocked. She could do with a mind like Shaw's, sharp and penetrating, on a case like this one. She ought to read the play again; she couldn't remember what he really thought of Mrs Warren's profession, probably praised her for earning a living.

Then the thought of that puritanical figure stalking round Waxy House amused her.

One by one the waxworks were being carried out,

each decently covered in a white shroud. Even thus covered they did not look dead, however: a leg stuck up here, an arm thrust out there, and the round curve of a bottom stood out as she was carried upside down. No lewd comments were made as they passed her and Drimwade, but she fancied that they were repressed and would burst out afterwards.

She moved up the stairs, Drimwade following. Rewley seemed to have disappeared.

The rooms, never large, looked smaller with the furniture pulled into the centre so that floors and walls could be investigated.

'There's a kind of rank feeling to this house,' said Drimwade suddenly. 'And I don't just mean the smell,' he added with force.

They had come up level with the big looking-glass on the wall. Square and solid in its gilt frame, it covered a large area of the wall on the staircase. Charmian could see her face in it, slightly distorted by the old glass. It was probably valuable; it looked antique.

The face in the mirror as it stared back at her looked tired and strained, pale, with hair untidy, not like a woman in command of anything. Drimwade, as he came up behind her, appeared as a sturdy countryman, a man out of a Shakespeare comedy. Comedy, mark you, she thought, not a tragedy. *A Midsummer Night's Dream* rather than *Macbeth*.

One of the policemen conducting the search, carefully white-robed so that the house was protected against him, came up the stairs.

'I want this big looking-glass taken down. Now,' said Charmian.

THE WOMAN WHO WAS NOT THERE

'Yes, ma'am. At once.' He turned away to get another searcher. The glass was heavy and would take some moving.

At last Drimwade allowed himself to put the question he had been bottling up all this time. 'What is it you are looking for, Miss Daniels? What do you expect to find?'

There came a shout from below. Rewley called: 'There's something here below. It needs looking at. Come on down.'

Charmian ran down the stairs. Rewley was standing at the door to the dining room. A line of floorboards had been pulled up; they followed the angle of those in the hall beneath which the body of the baby had been hidden. 'Very rotten,' explained Rewley, 'the whole area here is treacherous, which is why these boards were pulled up. Could have gone through and broken a leg. But look down, through the underpinnings . . . You can just see it – there's a room below.'

'I thought there might be,' said Charmian. 'I had a hunch.' She knelt down to study what she could see. Not much, but an electric bulb strategically placed showed a patch of stone-flagged floor. She could see nothing else, so she stood up. 'All these houses of this age had a basement . . . It was probably the kitchen.' She moved, dusting her hands on her skirt; she was past caring what she looked like. She smiled at Rewley. 'Good for you, finding it.'

'But how did anyone get down to it?'

'Let's wait and see,' she said.

Rewley accepted this enigmatic remark, but Drimwade, looking over his shoulder, said: 'I think you're wanted upstairs . . . that looking-glass. They must have it down.'

'Possibly. Or moved if not down.'

Now what does that mean? thought Rewley.

The man responsible for moving the looking-glass stood with his hand on it.

He put his fingers behind the gold rim and pulled. The looking-glass swung away.

Behind was a narrow flight of steps.

'It's a door,' he said. 'Leads on to a staircase.'

'Of course,' said Charmian. 'The back stairs. They had to be there.'

Rewley, Drimwade and the young policeman were crowded behind her, trying to get a look.

'Let's go down,' she said.

Rewley produced a torch. 'We'll need this. Let me go first.'

'You go first if you wish . . . but you won't need the torch. If you feel around, you'll find a switch, a nice modern switch.'

With some amusement she watched Rewley, his hand in a plastic glove, reach to the wall inside on the right of the door; he muttered something and then the staircase was lit, dimly but adequately.

'It wouldn't do to have it too bright,' said Charmian. 'People would see, and that was not desired.'

'But what was it used for?' asked Drimwade over her shoulder.

'I don't know that it was used much, but it was handy, a good thing to have in the circumstances.'

'What circumstances?'

She ignored that. 'And it was certainly made use of to frighten Fanny and me on the night we spent here.' She gave Rewley a little push. 'Down you go and I'll follow.'

They all trooped down the stairs.

At the bottom they found a square, stone-flagged room with streaky whitewashed walls, some patches cleaner and whiter and damper than others.

The old familiar smell was strong; she could work out some of its constituents now: new plaster, then fresh distemper, and mixed in with it the smell of disinfectant. Carbolic powder, by the smell. A hint of tobacco smoke... At last she had picked up the element that had worried her. Whoever used this room, and for what purpose, had smoked in the process.

She thought she could understand why, because underneath the smell of plaster and disinfectant was a scent more sickly. She observed that the wall had an uneven look to it.

'Someone has been using the house, coming in this way and going up the staircase.'

'I think so.'

Rewley had been looking around the room. 'How did he, or she, get in?'

'I expect there's a key to the front door, but it's not the entrance used as a rule by the killer, although he, or she,' Charmian added carefully 'must have made use of it when...' again she paused, 'any other visitors were brought in. They walked in.' She was beginning to build up the picture for them. She looked up the walls, walking around. 'I've been thinking about that. But up there is a grille in the wall.' She pointed to a high point near the ceiling. 'The earth has risen around Waxy House over the years . . . If you go outside, that grille will be about garden level and I'm sure it's less rusty that it looks. It could be lifted out and a person – man or woman, as you rightly say – could drop through.' She studied the wall. 'Two footholds there as well; you could get out as well as in. It's not far; this is a low-ceilinged little room. Must have been hell for the original poor slavey who lived in it. Slept in it as well, I guess.'

'So . . .' Drimwade spoke for the first time. 'What was the purpose of the gymnastics? What was the room used for?'

'The smell is a bit of a clue, to my mind,' said Charmian. 'Anyway, over to you. Open up the walls, go in where it's rough, that's my advice . . . Dig up the floor.'

Charmian sat in the police van, drinking coffee while she waited for news from those dismantling the basement. The demolition gang, she called them to herself. Drimwade and Rewley came and went.

Presently Rewley appeared silently in the door of the van. He nodded. 'You knew what we would find?'

Charmian stood up. 'Say that I expected it. How many?'

'One, so far. But there are indications of at least two other bodies down there.'

THE WOMAN WHO WAS NOT THERE

'I'm coming to see for myself.'

'It's not pleasant.'

'I've seen dead bodies before.'

Rewley was quiet for a moment, then he said: 'There's something horrible here . . . The first woman may not have been dead when she was walled up.'

Rewley led the way down the stairs. The room was now lit by a harsh, strong light, in which the searchers, their white suits neat and tidy, looked ill at ease, as if it was their fault what they had uncovered.

Another police surgeon had been called in, one not known to Charmian, and a pathologist had already arrived. Drimwade had been efficient. His face looked white and tired; the bright light drained everyone of colour.

'Dr Greenwade and Dr Ambrose,' he introduced them politely.

The two men of science were talking quietly to each other, but they stopped their conversation as Charmian walked up to the body.

The first, for there would be others, was embedded in the wall, like an erect mummy. Not mummified, though, the flesh still on the bones, recognizably a woman's face with a flow of slack hair. The skin was mottled blue and black, with here there patches of mould.

'We think she's bound to the wall, or she would fall forward.' said the pathologist, Dr Greenwade, a young man with bright red hair and a cheerful face. 'Indications of a belt round the waist . . . leather or rope. And something attached to the back of the neck. Fixed to hooks in the wall, I guess.'

'Needs time and some skill.'

'Yes, a practical chap, or chapess,' he added with careful political correctness. 'Wouldn't take strength, just skill.'

'Getting the body in here would take strength,' said Drimwade. 'Poor soul, I expect she was a pro.'

Charmian said: 'I don't think the body was pushed through that little window.' She nodded towards the wall. 'I guess she walked in, thinking she was just on the job.' Charmian moved to the middle of the room and looked around her. 'The killer has a key to this house, must have. An exit and an entrance, two ways in and out.' She nodded towards the further corner of the room: 'Another body there, I think.'

'I agree,' said Dr Greenwade. 'And another under the floor, to the right of where you're standing. In this light, you can see the stone flags have been raised. Burial there would not present the same technical difficulties as the wall.' Then he said: 'But I think this killer must have liked the idea of walling the victim up. Kind of medieval, isn't it?'

Or a gothic horror tale, Charmian thought. Mrs Radcliffe or Horace Walpole.

'Yes?' she encouraged Greenwade.

'I can't be sure, of course. I'll know more when I've had a look at the lungs, but I can see plaster dust up the nostrils and blood around the fingernails of the right hand.' He pointed to the one hand uncovered. 'She may well have been alive when she was walled up.'

A moment of silence followed. 'Makes you sick, doesn't it?'

'We will hope not,' said Greenwade. 'I shall know more when I do a full investigation . . . And she may have been unconscious; the movement of the hands could have been involuntary.'

'It's not an old person, anyway.' Charmian had been studying the face. 'This is quite a young woman.'

Drimwade nodded towards the excavators. 'Better get on with it . . . You won't stay, Miss Daniels?'

'I think not.' No good purpose could be served by being there.

'It'll take all night, I reckon.'

He was showing her to the stairs and then the door, and for once she was glad to go.

Rewley followed her out and towards her car.

'There's one thing we know about this killer. He, or she,' Charmian added carefully, 'must have strong hands.'

While all this activity had been going on in Leopold Walk, Angus Cairns had enjoyed his evening with Angela and Edward. His father had telephoned and agreed that he could spend the night there on the camp bed in the sitting room.

Made brave by all this, knowing he was not to be alone in the house but was here with two people who were being kind, he managed to tell Angela what was on his mind.

He sat up on the camp bed, in a striped pyjama jacket belonging to Edward (the trousers were hopelessly too big and not worn), holding a mug of Ovaltine, and told Angela.

'I saw, you see. I know what the person looks like.'

'Tell me,' said Angela, drinking Ovaltine herself.

'In black, with a bit of black stuff round the head so I could only see the eyes. Glistening.'

'Would you know this person again?'

'Might do . . . She'd know me.'

'She?'

'I thought it was a woman . . . The feet, you see. I could see high-heeled shoes.'

Angela thought. 'Tell you what. In the morning we'll go and see an old police officer I know. See what he thinks.'

One last question. 'This person,' she asked. 'Tall or short?'

Angus considered. 'Tall for a woman, very tall,' he said finally.

And on this bisexual note, the matter was left.

Angela settled Angus for the night, then went in to see Edward, who was also in bed. She told him what she had said to Angus.

After she had left him he was worried. Was it a good idea to go to Frank Felyx? He found himself thinking it was not.

Chapter Thirteen

The Final Hours

There was a message from her husband on the answerphone when Charmian got back to her house.

'Sorry not to be back...'

Well, I had noticed you weren't here, Charmian thought.

'But...'

Wasn't there a philosophical argument that said buts are constitutionally iffy? She had read it somewhere and it had struck her as a memorable phrase, destined to prepare you for life's disappointments. In other words, after a but look out for something you don't wish to hear.

'But this planning meeting looks like going on to the small hours, and then I have a follow-up tomorrow morning so I'll stay overnight...'

Planning what? She was never allowed to know. (Although, possessing her own channels of information, she could often guess.) I have my problems too, she thought.

'See you tomorrow evening.' She turned off the machine at that point. She was not sure what tomorrow evening would bring for her. Bodies and bodies, by the look of it.

She fed the cat, drank some milk, ate a sandwich of dry cheese, and went to bed. The cat came with her, pointing out wordlessly that the damp and chill of the night demanded a warm bed. Cats are not selfish, Charmian decided, as she eased herself round the firm, striped body, they just don't think of other animals.

She had meant to lie in bed to do some serious thinking about the bodies in Waxy House. Was Alicia going to turn up among them there, or was she still limping round in a homicidal rage?

And if Alicia was not the killer in black – because surely she could not be – then who was? Male or female?

Frank Felyx was a nuisance, if no more, she decided as sleep began to soften her thoughts. He knew or guessed more than he had told her. She would like to take him in for questioning and shake some answers out of him. Not allowed, of course, and Frank as a former police officer knew all the tricks anyway.

The cat began to snore, there was something soothing about the soft, rhythmical sound. Charmian drifted into sleep.

Soon she was dreaming. One of those dreams when you stagger beneath a load of luggage to catch a train which always recedes before you. There were the usual complications: it was, after all, a bus she was meant to catch – a coach, really, with Day Trip to Royal Windsor on the front. And, goodness, there was the Queen with a dog sitting in the front seat, smiling graciously. And that was Arthur Doby in the driver's seat, grinning through his skull. How had he become fleshless so soon?

THE WOMAN WHO WAS NOT THERE

The forensic experts would be able to explain that quick peeling away of the flesh. She was coming awake. For a moment she was awake; Dolly might have something to tell her from the forensics, although she could not remember why she thought that, and if, indeed, she did.

She fell back into sleep.

The Queen was no longer on the bus, and Charmian had once again lost her luggage. No, there it was on the coach. Except that it had turned into a set of little coffins. She had to retrieve the coffins, get the right bodies in the appropriate boxes and see they were named and buried decently. This was her job. She looked down at herself; she was covered in a long black robe which would make running for the coach difficult. If she had the feet for it. Something funny there too.

The bus drove away before she could get on it and Charmian woke up, thoroughly and completely this time, with that hollow feeling you get after restless sleep.

A grey dawn was crawling into the sky.

As if to welcome her into the day the telephone rang. It's Humphrey, she thought at once, and, with the dottiness of those just roused from a nightmare, thought, he's ringing up to say he's dead. Had an accident, is dying. Reason was coming back. Probably not Humphrey at all.

It was Rewley. 'It's early, I know, but the digging is over in Waxy House and I thought you'd like to know: the count is four bodies, all women. Two walled up, two in the floor.'

'How were they killed?'

'It looks as though they were strangled, by a cord in each case.'

'How long have they been dead?'

'The pathologist has to work on that side of things. He's got a lot of work all at once, but he guesses the last dead was about a year ago and the first possibly six or seven years. There may be some forensic details that will help.'

Charmian had been digesting all he had to say. 'So Alicia Ellendale is not among them?'

'No, on the evidence of the feet, they can't be Alicia. In any case, with the exception of one woman, who may have been the first killed, they were all younger women. Probably, although obviously we don't know yet, they are Phyllis Adams, Jane Fish, Mary Grey and Kathleen Mace.' He was reading the names out from a list in front of him. 'There's a lot more work to do.' Suddenly he sounded exhausted. 'And I need hardly tell you that by now there is a sizeable media contingent camped out round the corner. They can't get into Leopold Walk itself owing to the precautions that Drimwade took. I'm only frightened that they'll find the back way in.'

'There is one?'

'Yes, a network of tiny paths at the back through an ancient alley. The alley is old enough but the paths I should guess go back before the Normans... Run over the four back yards and onwards into what is now the brewery. It would be interesting to have aerial photographs to see if one could pick them up again, going towards the river and the Home Park.'

Charmian listened patiently, letting him run on.

THE WOMAN WHO WAS NOT THERE

She knew Rewley in this mood; it was a mark of his fatigue.

'So what are you going to do now?'

'Have a hot bath, breakfast and then get back to it. Shave, too; I'm beginning to look like the Old Man of the Woods.'

'And Drimwade?'

'He was still there. Can't bear to let go.'

The cat had jumped off the bed and was scrabbling at her arm. Breakfast time.

'I don't think it's just that with Drimwade,' said Charmian slowly. 'He really minds, it's got under his skin. I like him more than I thought.'

And he likes you, Rewley said to himself. Not that you've noticed. 'He'll hang around,' he said aloud.

'Thanks for ringing, Rewley.' She pushed the cat away from her arm. 'I'll be down there myself. But first I'm going to do as you do: hot bath and breakfast.' She was surprised to feel hungry. 'I'd like to think we were getting near the end of this affair.'

'It feels more like the beginning.'

'The dead do speak quite loudly sometimes.'

'This lot will have to shout,' said Rewley as he rang off.

Fanny was sitting by her bed in the small side ward where she had spent all the time since she was attacked, in company with a young woman who had undergone some mysterious operation either to improve her fertility or do away with it altogether, Fanny was not clear – she found the medical terms tossed across to her too hard to fathom. In her day, you either had them or you didn't, you didn't exactly leave it to nature but interference was modest. This girl did a lot of sleeping; hiding from the world was Fanny's diagnosis. She felt sorry for the young husband when he visited, as he did regularly.

She was surprised to see Charmian walk in. 'You've only just caught me. Good job you weren't any later, I'm going out today. Home.'

'It's not much after nine,' said Charmian.

'They get you up and out early in hospital. Always did and still do, that's one thing that hasn't changed.'

'I'll drive you home if you like.'

'No need, the girls are coming. Dorie, Paulina and Ethel.'

She sounded smug. 'Taxi.'

'Ah.' Too much to hope that that trio would not have heard about the bodies in Waxy House and be prepared to pass the news on with speed. 'There are certain developments that you ought to know about, but perhaps this isn't the time.' Fanny still looked very fragile.

Fanny arranged her skirt. 'You don't know much about hospitals and nurses if you think that I haven't already heard that there's been a body found in Waxy House.'

Charmian looked away.

'More than one body, then?' said Fanny sharply. 'Sometimes I can read you like a book. Well, really, it is my house.'

'All right, Fanny.'

'Trying to shield me. Don't bother.'

THE WOMAN WHO WAS NOT THERE

For answer, Charmian laid two lists in front of Fanny.

        Phyllis Adams   J. Birthday
        Jane Fish   T. Candleman
        Mary Grey   S. Claus
        Kathleen Mace

'Any of these names mean anything to you?'

Fanny studied first one list and then the other. 'No,' she said. 'Nothing.' Then she relented. 'Well, I might have known Kathleen Mace – not sure, but I could have done.' She pushed the paper away. 'She called herself something else then, not one real name among them, you can always smell it. I can, anyway, so much experience. Was my profession, after all.'

'I guessed that.' Charmian too had her experience. 'What about the other list?'

Fanny gave her back the list. 'No comment. As they say.'

'Well, that's something. Thank you.' Charmian picked up the two sheets. 'I think you have told me something.'

'Oh well, yes.' Fanny heaved a sigh. 'Perhaps there was a name there that meant something.' She pointed. 'That one. But only because Frank joked about it once.'

'Frank Felyx.' Charmian was wrathful. 'He's everywhere. Do you know that in seventeenth-century France there was a man called *l'éminence grise*', the grey excellency. He was behind all intrigues, pulled all the strings. I'm beginning to feel that Frank is our *éminence grise*.'

245

'If you say so,' said Fanny. 'Although I haven't the least idea what you're talking about.' She looked about her with amusement. 'One of the nurses on night duty said that she had heard there was a severe risk of infection from the house. Of course, she didn't know it was my house.' Or did she? Fanny considered the possibility. People could be so envious of a property owner. 'She said she'd heard a rumour that there was a plague pit in the garden, but that's rubbish.'

'There is no plague in Waxy House and no danger of any infection except of wickedness.' She bent down to kiss Fanny's cheek, on which a light dusting of rouge had already appeared. Fanny was certainly on the mend. 'I'll come round to see you later, Fanny. Goodbye.'

'It's the white coats on the coppers doing the digging,' Fanny called after her. 'Of course they make people think there's something infectious.'

Charmian did not answer this gambit. Fanny was sophisticated enough to know that the white garments were to protect the remains being dug up from the diggers and not the other way round. Forensic science demanded that no particles be passed around like chocolates.

Otherwise, what Fanny had said was supported by the crowd at the end of Leopold Walk. Not much could be seen by them because big screens had been set up around the house precisely to stop unseemly gaping. Inside the barriers the proprietors of the three business houses of Leopold Walk were conferring. Charmian guessed they were wondering whether to take a holiday or start business for the day. Mr Bacon was talking away to Chris Fenwick, who was listening with a frown, while Harry Aden was staring straight ahead, not paying much attention but not looking cheerful. In fact, not one of them looked cheerful, and quite right, Charmian thought. Two of them were suspects and one of them was due for some heavy questioning. Drimwade had already reported that the movements of all three on the day of Doby's death were hard to check: Bacon had been out, alone, viewing a country property so that he had left in the early morning; Chris Fenwick had been working, on his own except for his drawing board, and Harry Aden had only his mother to testify where he was. She was a biased witness.

Charmian walked through the crowd and into Waxy House. Inside was Superintendent Drimwade, a Detective Inspector March, whom she knew by sight (keen eager beaver, Rewley had called him, but this was when March had been going out with Dolly Barstow), and Sergeant Jacaponi. Their faces and air of consultation mirrored the trio outside.

'One more turned up,' said Drimwade to her. 'Thought we'd done. In the floor.'

Dr Cairns had appeared again, and was just closing his medical bag. 'Young female, dead, very dead,' he shrugged. 'Up to you now. They can all be moved as soon as you want.' He looked pinched and worried. He saw Charmian then and gave her a nod. 'I must talk to you.' His voice was urgent. 'Personal.'

Charmian nodded. 'In a minute,' and to Drimwade

she said: 'So you've found five now? Any identification?'

'No.' Drimwade shook his head. 'Not Ellendale. Got both her feet, this one, so no help there. We reckon this was the first done. Lowest down. Where he started off.'

'You're sure the killer is a man?'

'Got to be,' said Drimwade, with deep conviction.

Gender coming in again, thought Charmian. A really evil serial killer has to be a man. Women have sexual fantasies too. Think of Nurse Brownrigg, whipping her apprentice to death. Something more there than sheer brutality.

'I'll talk to Dr Cairns, then I'll go downstairs and have a look round . . .'

'We haven't found any bodies upstairs,' said Drimwade with gloom, 'but there is always time. Checking for fingerprints all over, of course, and all forensic fragments.' He did not sound hopeful.

Cairns was waiting for Charmian outside. 'It's the boy. He's missing.'

'Angela telephoned me this morning to say she was taking him to see her grandfather.'

'Yes, Frank Felyx.'

'She said she had permission, but she wanted to tell me.'

'She did have my permission,' Cairns said. 'She got it from me. She said the boy had something important to say and she wanted advice. I told her she could but also to go to you.'

'So she did.'

THE WOMAN WHO WAS NOT THERE

'I don't know what it is he could have to say that he couldn't say to me.'

'He may have tried. Angela said the boy thought he might recognize the killer.'

Cairns threw his hands up. 'I can't believe she could be so stupid as to take the boy there.'

Charmian pushed down the thought that Angela wanted to confront Angus with her grandfather. 'I don't know exactly what was in her mind; I expect nothing except her grandfather knew a lot about crime and could give good advice.'

'And now they're both missing. She said she'd have him at school in good time. But he isn't there. He never turned up. I've rung Felyx and he's not answering.'

'I don't think Angus will come to any harm.' Inside she was cursing Frank, Angela and even Angus. 'Frank Felyx is not the killer. You go home now and you might find them both there. Or the boy might be at school.'

She walked with Dr Cairns to the car, still making noises of reassurance. Mr Bacon was outside, talking to Chris Fenwick and Harry Aden.

'Is Angela in your office?'

'Gave her the day off, we're closed today. I rang everyone when I heard what was going on here. I hope you lot know what you're doing; it's bad for business, especially my business. Is it true you keep turning up bodies?'

'Is that what people are saying? There have been discoveries, yes, but I'm sure you understand I can't talk about it.'

She noticed that Cairns had not driven off but was sitting in his car, apparently deep in thought.

'Has your wife turned up, Mr Fenwick?'

He shook his head.

'I do need to speak to her.'

'I don't see why. She didn't know Alicia Ellendale.'

Charmian found a nerve throbbing in her temple, bringing with it the hint that although she did not have a headache now, there might be one coming.

'We haven't found Alicia yet.' She turned to look at Harry Aden. 'Now you three are all here together, I want to tell you that I will be ordering a search of your back gardens.'

'We hardly have gardens,' said Fenwick. 'Just little patches. No walls or fences to speak of, long since fallen down.'

'Big enough. And later I may possibly institute a search of your houses.'

'Why?' asked Harry Aden.

'Well, as neighbours to this house, you three might have the best access to it.' As Fenwick had boldly said: there were no real boundaries at the back.

'By that token, I'm the nearest,' said Harry Aden.

'I'm open-minded,' said Charmian.

'Glad to hear it.' He spoke seriously.

'Will you three gentlemen please wait here for me? I'll be back.'

At last she had seen what she expected and needed to see. She walked over to the car. 'Dr Cairns, you can stop worrying. Here comes your son with Frank Felyx.'

Frank, side by side in a companionable way with Angus, was pushing through the crowd and being admitted by the police constable in charge, who had his orders.

THE WOMAN WHO WAS NOT THERE

'Frank, Angus, why are you so late?'

'I was giving this young chap a good breakfast.' Frank sounded more cheerful than for some time past. 'The food my grand-daughter hands out wouldn't feed a bird.'

'Bacon and eggs,' said Angus. 'Yum.' He too looked in better spirits.

'Dad won't be pleased, not when I tell him what a great time I'm having,' and Angus led the way to the car.

Charmian went back into Waxy House. She walked down the stairs to the terrible basement where the four bodies were being zipped into decent black bags and loaded on to gurneys. The fifth was still being photographed while awaiting the first survey of the pathologist.

A young, twisted little face and a curled-up body, foetus-like. Something about the soil in this place seemed to slow decay. The flesh was recognizable still. She was completely clothed in dark jeans and what had been a white shirt.

'Coloured girl,' said Drimwade, who had followed her down. 'Only a kid, strangled like the rest. At least she was dead when she was buried. Remains of a cigarette in the earth there too, someone left it. She's the missing student, we think.'

Charmian stood back. No doubt about it; the throbbing in her head was worse. Had she eaten any breakfast? She couldn't remember. So many ideas had been rushing through her mind since she woke up that she had thought more of telephoning this one and that.

'I want one man to come with me to go over the

next-door house and then the next one, Aden's and then Fenwick's.'

'Not the accountant chap, Bacon?'

'I'm not so interested in him.'

'I'll come myself,' said Drimwade.

They stood in the ground-floor room where Harry Aden stored his equipment. Charmian had extracted him from the trio, told the others to wait their turn, and entered the house with him. It was a smaller place than Waxy House, but immaculately clean.

'You have to keep this stuff spotless,' Aden explained. 'Dust and dirt don't agree with it.'

The house was warm and dry too. 'I prefer it that way,' he explained with a touch of humour. 'But it suits the software too.'

A family may once have lived in this house, but there was no sense of that left; it was a workplace. The floors were bare wood, unpolished but once again very clean. All the woodwork of the house was white. At the windows hung blinds which could be pulled down against the sun. The room on the middle floor was where Harry Aden had banks of screens besides all the other instruments that he needed. Several telephones seemed to be necessary with fax machines attached. The house was totally impersonal.

'I do look out of the window sometimes,' he said, reading her mind. 'Just to see the world is there.'

'But you didn't see anything that worried you about next door?'

'I don't worry when I work.'

'That's no answer.'

'The best I can do.'

Followed by Drimwade, she marched briskly through each room. The top floor was empty. 'Don't use it,' said Aden who had come with them.

'You don't smoke?' asked Charmian as they walked down the stairs.

'Never have. I'm asthmatic, wouldn't suit me. I eat sweets, though, and that's what gives me this round and cuddly look.'

'I don't think I'd call you a cuddly man, Mr Aden. I think you're sharp as well as highly intelligent—'

'That's the computers, I suppose,' he broke in.

'Not entirely, just how I read you. Intelligent, observant, although you claim not, and exceedingly unhappy.'

He was silent. 'Caroline Fenwick didn't come to me. I don't know where she is. I think she may be in trouble. She knew I loved her, I had begun to think we might do something about it. But she went off, didn't even say goodbye.'

'Was she normal about sex?'

'I don't know,' he said in an unhappy voice. 'What is normal? Am I normal, I feel normal to me, but who am I to judge? But we never had sex together. It didn't happen. Perhaps that wasn't normal.'

'Maybe not,' said Charmian. 'Did she smoke?'

'Sometimes.'

Drimwade had been silent all this time, but he looked sharply at Charmian when he heard this question.

As they walked down the stairs, he said: 'I see what you're getting at but I don't see how.'

'Not sure I see myself.'

He followed her out of the door. 'How's your headache?'

With surprise, Charmian said: 'Coming on. How did you know I had one?'

'Because I've got one myself,' said Drimwade with dignity.

When they got out into the street again, Charmian went over to the car. 'Frank, Angus, why don't you go for a walk in the gardens; they run into each other and it makes a pleasant little walk. There's a couple of men searching the gardens but you can ignore that.'

Angus got out of the car with Frank holding his elbow and shepherding him past Chris Fenwick. 'Walkies,' Frank said, 'Think your dad would buy you a dog?'

Angus turned to wave to his father, who waved back, calling out that he would wait. They left him hunched over the wheel, muttering a dog, there had to be a dog.

Charmian led Chris Fenwick round his house, which was plain but neat, an architect's workplace. On one wall was a reproduction of a great dark Poussin: Christ and the Introduction of the Eucharist. She looked at it with interest. Then she took him into the garden where two uniformed men were slowly quartering the ground, head down. 'What are they doing?' he demanded.

'Just looking. People leave traces when they pass, you know. They can be useful. It's called the Locard principle. Tell me, did your wife wear high-heeled shoes?'

Fenwick went still. 'Sometimes.'

'Useful to know. Did she take her shoes with her when she left?'

He was breathing more easily now. 'I daresay. I haven't looked. Does it matter?'

'Might do.'

Down the garden Angus and Frank were pacing the grass too, staring down at the garden. There was a large shed at the bottom.

'That your shed?'

'The last tenant put it there, so I suppose it is mine.'

'Do you use it at all?'

'My wife did. She grew a lot of vegetables; we have a small allotment. My wife's, really, I'm not great with fruit and veg.'

'You must know where she is. Why won't you tell me?'

'When she gets in touch with me, then of course I'll tell her you want to see her.'

With determination, Charmian said: 'It's important to me to find her. We will find her, trust me.' She stopped and turned to face him. 'Come on, tell me. It'll be better all round if she's found without any fuss.'

Harry Aden walked across to them, angry. 'There's these men tramping all over my garden. What do they think I keep there?'

'I don't know, Mr Aden. Not yet.'

'Perhaps they don't know themselves.'

'I've explained to Mr Fenwick here that scraps and traces can be very important forensic evidence.'

'For God's sake, stop calling me Mr Fenwick. Chris will do. Or nothing – yes, nothing would be best.'

'Mr Nothing,' said Aden.

Charmian said: 'Chris, I'd like to look in that shed your wife uses.'

'I don't know why you're so interested.'

She took her time before answering. Words were important. Nervous tension and fear were her weapons.

'There's a theory going around that your wife, dressed in black, dropped Alicia Ellendale's shoe with the foot in it near the river. There is an addition to this: that still dressed in black but this time limping like Alicia, she killed the coach driver . . . Remember him? There was an idea that it was Alicia, somehow surviving, but I don't believe that. But I have to find Alicia, because that was what I was asked to do. And that leads me to your wife.'

'What possible motive could my wife have for behaving like that?' His hands, cigarette stained and sinewy, were clenched.

Charmian shook her head at him. 'It's what I would like to ask her. But the scenario that has been suggested to me . . .' She let her eyes take in Frank and Angus, who were watching them at a distance. Frank had his hand on the boy's shoulder, restraining or supporting him. 'It has been suggested that your wife is bisexual. She may have hated women like Alicia who traded their sex for money.'

'I'll fight that idea to the death,' said Harry Aden, almost in tears. 'She's a lovely woman, she couldn't kill.'

THE WOMAN WHO WAS NOT THERE

'I need to see her for myself,' said Charmian. She looked at Chris Fenwick. 'You could be hiding her. Let's have that shed open.'

'She has the key.'

Charmian nodded to one of the searchers. 'He has broad shoulders; he can break down that door.'

Harry Aden said: 'I have a key . . . She gave it to me. We met there once or twice.' He avoided looking at Fenwick.

'If you have it on you, then open the door.'

Silently, Harry produced the key from an upper pocket.

'Carry it next to your heart, do you?' snarled Fenwick. 'I could kill you for this.'

The door swung open. It was a large shed with carefully arranged vegetable racks. It smelt earthy and of potatoes with a hint of onions.

A canvas armchair and a camp bed with rolled-up blankets lined one wall. There was a desk beside it and opposite a very large white freezer.

'Lived here, did she?' asked Charmian.

White and angry, Chris Fenwick said: 'Of course not, but it was a business with her – a small one, but she enjoyed it. She grew it all in an allotment, stored it here, then she sold the produce in the market off a stall.'

Charmian opened the freezer. Packets of frozen peas, neatly labelled, filled a plastic tray.

She lifted the tray. Underneath was the small figure of a woman, legs drawn up. From the ankle there were no feet. It was Alicia.

'I see why the feet went,' she said. 'Alicia wouldn't

have fitted in the freezer if she'd still had her feet. I ought to have guessed there was a practical reason.'

Harry Aden staggered away to the door. 'I'm going to be sick.'

Charmian put a restraining hand on him. 'Before you do that, I want you and Chris here to lift up Alicia.'

'No, no, I couldn't.'

'You may be right. I ought to get the professionals in here first, to do it right. Let me just move her hair aside.'

She drew a pair of white gloves out of her pocket and gently moved the dead woman's hair. Underneath were more vegetables, but they were lightly packed and she could see beneath to another body. She pushed one of the bags aside and saw a woman's face. The eyes stared back at her, clouded and pale. Younger than Alicia and longer dead.

'Chris . . . I must ask you to identify your wife.'

At the door Harry Aden was retching and gasping. 'Please,' he was muttering, 'please, please.'

'Yes,' said Charmian. 'Other people can be bisexual, can dress up in black and learn to limp like a woman with a foot cut off at the ankle.'

'Are you going to arrest him?' asked Chris, flexing his hands, 'or do you want me to kill him for you?'

'No, let's go outside. I have someone out there who might know a face. Come on, Harry, brace yourself.' She pushed Aden out into the garden and beckoned towards Frank and Angus.

'I have some more thoughts to share. Cigarette smoke, a name in the list of members of a club which collected coins or pretended to do so while having other interests... One of the men went by the nickname Santa Claus... Sounded a bit like you, Harry, but you don't smoke and I smelt smoke when someone came up the back staircase to frighten Fanny that night.' She turned towards Chris Fenwick. 'It was not your wife, because she was dead too, but you smoke; I saw the stain on your fingers just now. I could smell it on your clothes. And the nickname Candleman could be you, Mr Nothing, Mr Fenwick. Because a wick is part of a candle, the bit that burns.'

Angus, supported by Frank, came up to them. He stared from Harry Aden to Chris Fenwick, then he nodded.

'He thinks it's you, Chris,' said Charmian. 'He thinks he saw you by the river.'

Chris Fenwick sprang at her, hands outstretched; he had them round her throat. 'I am not Mr Nothing, nor Candleman. I am not building a church, I am a church. *Christus natus hodie*, my name is Christ. Sinners must die and go to hell. I must kill you just like the rest of all the other women.'

She felt the fingers tighten round her throat and the colour fade out of the world. This way death came quickly.

'I had to make him lose his head... At that time there was no real evidence against him,' she said. But she would rake it in now, forensic evidence would do the job, but everyone, here and in London, whose path had crossed the Fenwicks', would be questioned until all significant details were milked. Charmian was in her office with Rewley and Dolly Barstow. 'Just speculation and a boy's observation. It wasn't a case...'

'He could have killed you,' said Superintendent Drimwade from the corner of the room, where he was sitting bolt upright in a hard chair. 'I thought we'd lost you; you don't know what you looked like, slumped on the grass.'

Charmian put her hands to her bruised throat. 'I'd taken the precaution of having two officers close at hand, that was no accident. And I was sure you would save my life.' She smiled at him.

'If I could have got there in time.'

'Alicia Ellendale was missing – I was looking for her, alive or dead – but I realized early on that there was another missing woman. The woman who wasn't there. Caroline Fenwick, Chris Fenwick's wife. She was spoken of but never seen. Away, I was told.'

Drimwade coughed. 'I've been talking to Harry Aden. He says that he believes she had discovered her husband's connection with the numismatists' porno group and was in touch with Arthur Doby, which may have been why Doby was killed.'

'I think Doby was about to tell all he knew to the police,' put in Dolly Barstow. 'And there was certainly an attempt to make him out to be the murderer by planting Alicia's shoe in the bus station... The sergeant thinks Doby was worried about his part in it... Bringing those working girls to Windsor for what amounted to execution.' She sneezed.

'Bad cold you've got,' said Charmian.

Drimwade went on: 'Aden thinks she was going to tell him, and he believes she had begun to suspect her husband's part in the disappearance of the women. Maybe she went into Waxy House itself. Aden knew she was scared and he thought at first that she had simply run away, from him as much as anyone. He didn't like that.'

'I don't think their relationship was as platonic as he made out,' said Charmian. 'I did notice the bed in the shed. And it had been used, even if the blankets were rolled up. If Fenwick knew that, and I guess he did, it may have been one touch of revenge to put his wife in the freezer. A nasty touch of irony. Alicia, poor soul, had to have her feet severed before he could get her in.'

'Aden says that Caroline was a very good architect and her husband depended on her professionally.'

'But not sexually, and she knew what he was from her joke to Frank when she was buying the big black overcoat – for her husband. She knew he was going to wear it.'

'None so mixed up as folks,' said Drimwade. 'I wonder why he left a sovereign in Waxy House. I mean it gave us a clue, something to follow up.'

'I can understand that. It was his sign; a sovereign and he was the ultimate sovereign. Like most of these killers he wanted to be known... Possessed, and not by the Devil like the Son of Sam, but by something holy.'

'Very strange to bring the girls down from London. I think we'll need to go into the numismatist group more thoroughly to see what we can find there. Doby brought them down, for pay, no doubt, and the girls were paid. Recruited in London and he offered good pay to them, I daresay.'

'Half before and half afterwards... Only there never was a second payment; they were dead. And he probably took the first payment back as well,' said Rewley. 'And an architect too.' He sounded sad; he had always admired architects. 'But I suppose his profession explained his cleverness with Waxy House.'

Charmian nodded. 'I realized pretty soon that an architect would be interested in Waxy House. The whole place fascinated him and, of course, he had to try to keep Fanny out, he couldn't have her in there finding what he had been up to. Perhaps he wouldn't have turned into what he was if he hadn't known Waxy House.'

'Isn't it odd,' said Dolly, 'that no one picked up what a strange, mad person he was? One shoe with a foot near Runnymede, not well hidden at all, easily found, as it turned out, and then one in the bus station. Odd, you know.'

'Worried me,' said Charmian. 'But I think he half wanted to display that foot and shoe, needed it found, somehow. Psychosis, I suppose. The other shoe, like the sovereign in the house, both could point at Doby, whom he hated. You have to remember we're talking about a seriously disturbed man.'

Dolly nodded. 'And why did he go for the London working girls? What about the locals?'

Charmian had a sudden and vivid picture of what had gone on: the girls brought from London, not often because after all even Fenwick did not desire death all the time and perhaps Doby had to find a girl who would travel. Perhaps it went with the moon, she thought, or his hormone levels. Hamlet knew a thing or two about the ups and downs of madness. Fenwick must have been normal, if you could call it that, some or most of the time. But getting madder as he enjoyed death more. Doby must have begun to wonder. Well, they knew he had done, hence his death. Did Doby ever see inside Waxy House with its dust? And did Fenwick enjoy the dust as part of his macabre pleasure? He only used the basement for the real stuff.

She became aware that the others were waiting for her to speak. 'I suppose he fancied playing an away game,' she said. 'Perhaps a London girl did him down. Alicia could have told a tale there, I expect. I imagine she acted as a bit of a go-between before he killed her. Maybe she was going to talk. We might get something out of Frank there, if he'll talk. I guess they had a relationship.' She added quickly, 'Frank may have guessed a lot at the end, but he's no killer, and there is no reason to believe he was involved in any way.'

'He'll need to talk a bit, though,' said Drimwade. 'And I'd like to know why no one suspected Fenwick.'

'Aden did eventually,' said Charmian. 'And as for what other people noticed, well, it's not all that strange. The Yorkshire Ripper seemed a nice, ordinary bloke, and probably even the first one, Jack the Ripper, must have done. He was never picked up, anyway. Unless someone tucked him away in a private asylum. I suppose Fenwick was over the top towards the end. He'll be found unfit to plead, I guess. I blame the house. It played the same part that working in the cemetery did for the Yorkshire Ripper, triggered something deep inside. It has a lot to answer for, that place. I shall never forget the smells.'

Dolly said: 'Smells were important all the way through. Dave Edwards has let me know that there is forensic evidence from both the cabs that Fenwick used to travel out to where Doby lived. Flecks of dried fish glue. He used it to stick layers of extra soles on his right foot to build up the shoe so the left one had to limp. He wasn't going to cut off his foot or make himself too uncomfortable, he just made one leg longer.' She wondered if Alicia's other foot would ever turn up? Buried or eaten in the river by a rat. She shivered. And went on: 'Fanny says she never knew who it was who attacked her and she isn't sure why it happened.'

'He wanted her out of the way. That was why he tried to frighten her with those tricks with dolls, moving them around. She was gullible there, but you have got to hand it to her; she's going to turn the place into a museum, all the keener now she knows how valuable the dolls are, and she hopes to get the tourists in. Adults only, of course.'

'That ought to bring them in,' said Dolly. 'Waxy House, the House of Sex and Death. She can't fail.'

And the house sign, two shoes, each with a severed foot, thought Charmian.